Terror on Every Side!

THE LIFE OF JEREMIAH

VOLUME 5 – No Remedy

Mark Morgan

Bible Tales

www.BibleTales.online

Published in Australia by Bible Tales Online.
www.BibleTales.online

**Terror on Every Side! The Life of Jeremiah
Volume 5 – No Remedy**

ISBN (Paperback): 978-1-925587-04-3
ISBN (Hardcover): 978-1-925587-07-4
ISBN (eBook): 978-1-925587-14-2

Last updated: 19 February 2021

Cover picture: Jerusalem from the Mount of Olives
by Frederick Edwin Church (1870).

Free Download

Paul in Snippets

A 109-page PDF novelette by Mark Morgan.

The life of Paul painted from the Acts of the Apostles.

Get your free copy of *Paul in Snippets* when you sign up for the Bible Tales mailing list. As well as the eBook, you will receive a weekly email newsletter with micro tales, informative articles and special offers.

Visit **https://www.BibleTales.online/free-pins**

www.BibleTales.online

To my ever-patient wife, Ruth.

Acknowledgements and thanks

In 2014, I prompted my daughter Heidi to write a Bible-based story. Her response was that I should show her how! This is my attempt to do so.

Particular thanks go to Ruth, my wife, who helped me find time to write, patiently read what I wrote, and humoured me when I spent inordinate amounts of time on research into minute details.

Feedback from early readers and subscribers has improved the story greatly, so I thank them. No manuscript is ever without errors, but these early readers helped eliminate most typos, bad grammar and uncomfortable usage. Cathy, my oldest daughter has tirelessly undertaken the thankless task of proof reading the entire manuscript more than once. Thanks, Cathy.

My son Chris has also helped with various technical details and his excellent reading has made the audio book a pleasure to listen to. I never expected to enjoy listening to anything I had written, but Chris achieved this.

A request

I have a request to make of all readers: if you find any errors; typos, spelling errors, poor grammar, unkempt use of vocabulary, or, most importantly, errors of fact where the story misrepresents the Bible, please let me know. I can't correct printed books, but electronic versions and any new printed editions can be fixed.

VOLUME FIVE

No Remedy

Contents

"Terror on Every Side!"

For I hear the whispering of many—
terror on every side!—
as they scheme together against me,
as they plot to take my life.

A psalm of David: Psalm 31:13

For I hear many whispering.
Terror is on every side!
"Denounce him! Let us denounce him!"
say all my close friends,
watching for my fall.
"Perhaps he will be deceived;
then we can overcome him
and take our revenge on him."

Jeremiah 20:10

Chapter 1

Away from death

588 BC – the 10th year of King Zedekiah

"Get up, and get out," ordered the guard, gesturing to the open door, where another guard could be seen waiting.

"What's the hurry?" I moaned.

"Just do what you're told. We'll tell you what's happening as we go."

"Will I be going outside? How cold is it? When will…."

"Oh, stop asking questions! Get up and get out, or I'll help you along with my spear."

I stood slowly and stumbled towards the door. Catching hold of the doorpost, I steadied myself, groaning, then bent over double as an agonising cough shook me.

"Get a move on. We don't have all day."

I couldn't answer. I couldn't move. At that moment, I might even have thanked him if he had lost patience and killed me with his spear.

Eventually, the coughing relaxed its grip enough for me to open my eyes and slowly move again.

"Take it easy, Jeremiah," said the guard from outside. "Come when you are ready."

"He doesn't deserve any sympathy, Vaniah," said the guard who had been haranguing me. "After all, he hasn't shown any for all the people who have died because of his treachery."

"Come on, Kallai, you know it's not Jeremiah's fault that Nebuchadnezzar has attacked us. He's attacking everyone."

"And so is Jeremiah. Didn't you hear about Hananiah the prophet? And now it's his own brother!"

"I heard about Hananiah, of course, but did Jeremiah really kill him?"

"He put a curse on him!"

"I can get a hundred men representing almost as many different gods or goddesses to put a curse on someone – but it doesn't mean much. Does Jeremiah really have the power to make curses happen, does he?"

"Well, I doubt it, but maybe he gives them a little helping hand with a bit of poison here and there."

"I have no power for such curses," I said, speaking slowly and with difficulty, "but Yahweh, the God of Israel, does. He cursed Hananiah for his lies and then fulfilled his curse."

"You were the one who spoke the curse, so don't blame God!" snarled Kallai. "And now you've killed your brother too."

"That's going a bit far, I reckon," said Vaniah. "I don't like Jeremiah's message any more than anyone else, but blaming him for everything bad that happens doesn't make sense."

"Anyway, I'm sick of arguing about it. Let's get him out of here and cleaned up."

I couldn't help putting a grimy hand to my face, my fingers feeling the dirt that covered it too. It would be good to get clean, but why the urgency? Despite my exhaustion, I was beginning to get suspicious about the entire affair.

"What for?" I asked.

"Don't ask any more questions, just do it." He struck at me as he spoke, sending me staggering back against the wall of my cell.

Vaniah hastily came between us and offered me his arm to lean on. "Kallai, there's no point in hurrying him out if he drops dead on the way because of how you treat him."

Slowly I recovered my balance and, leaning on Vaniah's arm, plodded slowly from the cell.

They marched me out of the vaulted chamber and took me to a room where I could wash.

"It hardly seems worth wasting precious water on a traitor like you," said Kallai sourly, "but those are our orders: clean you up and take you to the High Priest's house."

Slowly, I scrubbed off the accumulated dirt, reflecting on my situation as I did so. Why should I be taken to the High Priest's house? Was I to see my nephew, Seraiah, the new High Priest? It was hard to really accept that my nephew was old enough to be the High Priest. Time moves quickly.

The cold water revived me, but I still felt terribly weak as I put on the clean clothes the guards had given me.

"Hurry up," urged Kallai as we walked out of the house together. It was clear that I was not going to be set free – Kallai kept a grip on me at all times, but carefully avoided giving me any support. If I had collapsed on the paving, he would have cheered.

Slowly we made our way to the High Priest's house, and it was only when we arrived that it became clear that I had been called to help perform the duties necessary to bury my brother, Azariah. Suddenly I understood that when the news of my brother's death had come to me that morning, I had been one of the first to hear it. From the way it had been told me, and the delays I had experienced in hearing earlier news, I had assumed that it had happened days or weeks before. Instead, it appeared that just that morning, Azariah had arisen as usual and gone to the temple to make some arrangements for collecting the annual rent paid by several idolatrous cults for the right to have altars and idols in its courts. An hour later he had returned, saying that he felt a little strange. He went to lie down, and a short time later was found dead on his bed by a servant.

"I am not going in," I said to Vaniah.

"Why not?"

"Yahweh has told me not to take part in mourning."

"Nonsense! You won't go because you have no respect for the temple or the priests – even the High Priest," said Kallai.

"Not true. I must obey Yahweh. Even when my father died, back in the days of Josiah, I did not go in to mourn or bury him."

At that moment, my brother Gemariah came down the steps. "Who are you people? What do you want?" he asked.

"We are guards from the prison in the house of Jonathan, sir," answered Kallai. "Jehucal the son of Shelemiah told us to bring Jeremiah here, sir, to help with the burial of your brother. But now he is refusing to go in."

"Jeremiah?" My brother looked at me in shock – clearly he had not recognised me. He put a hand on my shoulder and looked into my face. "Is it really you, Jeremiah?"

"Yes."

"You look terribly ill. Where have you been?"

"In prison."

"But you were going out to see that land in Anathoth, weren't you? We knew from Mother that you had left, but that was all we knew. Mother was worried, but Azariah and I just assumed that you must have gone off somewhere on that work of yours. Then the Chaldeans came back and we couldn't do any more to check."

"They stopped me at the gate." I wanted to continue, to ask about Mother, but speaking only the few words I had spoken had left me exhausted.

"The officials were concerned that he was defecting to the Chaldeans, sir," interrupted Kallai.

"And he has been locked up all through the winter?"

"Yes, sir."

"And not fed very much, from the look of him."

"Nothing unusual, sir. We don't overfeed criminals. Or traitors."

"Nor my brother, either, it seems. Can't you tell that he is sick?"

"So was Hananiah the prophet, sir, if you will remember. Jeremiah didn't seem to care about him."

"Look, I don't have time to keep arguing with you, but once I have buried my older brother, I will see what I can do about my younger one." He looked back at me again and spoke more gently than he had done for several years. "Are you coming in, Jeremiah?"

"No. Yahweh said 'no mourning'."

"Oh, yes. I remember. Your stubbornness makes it hard for anyone to help you, you know."

"If he's not coming in, then we might as well take him away again, sir," said Kallai.

"I suppose so. You said that he was in Jonathan's house, didn't you?"

"Yes. On the orders of the officials, sir – the king's friends."

We left and walked slowly back to Jonathan's house, Kallai trying to hurry me up at every step.

❧

The death of my brother reminded me of my own mortality.

How long might I have left of my own life? True, Azariah was ten years older than I was, but I was already 55 years old, and my father had died at only 57. The way that I was feeling, it seemed quite likely that I, too, would be dead before long.

Would Gemariah be able to do anything about my situation? Would he really try?

I found that I didn't care very much either way, although I already had more desire to continue to live than I had felt that morning.

My brother was dead, a new High Priest had already been chosen and his ordination had begun. Time really was marching on. Azariah had been High Priest since the twentieth year of Josiah – and that was now 33 years ago! It took me a while to work out just how old my nephew Seraiah was, but in the end I concluded that he must be about 37 years old.

I stopped and thought: How did I feel about my brother? We had never got on well, but after all, a brother is a brother. My father had always favoured his firstborn, and Azariah had been closer in temperament to him than either Gemariah or I had been. I didn't hate him, but I didn't respect him either. My main feelings against him related to the way in which he had carried out his job as Yahweh's High Priest, and it is probably best not to go into details about that. He cannot defend his actions now.

Seraiah was taking over in a time of great difficulty for the nation. Whether he accepted it or not, all that could be expected was the final destruction of Jerusalem, and with it, the temple. Somebody had to be High Priest when that happened, but I was glad that it wasn't me. Seraiah's son, Jehozadak, was 16 years old at that point – too young to be a priest, and not likely to ever be one, even if he survived the coming desolation.

Having given my mind a little free rein in criticising others, I moved quite naturally on to the greater question which had been troubling me all through the winter as I suffered in my cell: how did I feel about God? I had been discontented with what was happening to me. God had promised me that he would care for me, as long as I remained strong in presenting his truth to my nation. But as my imprisonment dragged on, I began to feel that my nation was prevailing, and that God was no longer with me in the same way that he had been. I have to admit that I was blaming God for my troubles and my self-pity.

39 years of work as a prophet, and what was my reward? I was a hated outcast locked in a dungeon, in a city surrounded by an army that would soon destroy not only the city but my entire nation. It felt too much to bear.

Yet I still couldn't quite give up. My brother Gemariah – the brother I had always preferred – would do something to help me. Maybe his antagonism had eased. Maybe we could be friends again; maybe he would listen to God's warnings. All this takes much less time to describe than it took to work its way slowly through my mind. My body was weak and full of pain, and any thought was a major effort. I wondered whether I was dying, and maybe I was. I have no doubt that I would have died if I had stayed in that prison much longer. But despite my doubts, God was still taking care of me.

Then suddenly, as I brooded there alone, wondering what would become of me, a familiar tingling began to spread through me. Never before had I felt so unfit to encounter the presence of God. Yet the feeling spread through me, the fire ignited and a voice spoke.

☙

My oldest brother was buried that day, and my nephew Seraiah was to be the last High Priest to serve in Solomon's temple. If only we had kept our side of the agreement and stayed close to God as a nation, we would have been more worthy of God's promise that his name would be in the temple forever. But over the centuries, we had not done so, and in the end God had left the house that was called by his name.[1] Soon the empty shell would be knocked down.

Gemariah arranged Azariah's burial, making himself unclean by so doing. The rest of his efforts that day were

---

[1] See Ezekiel 9:3 and Ezekiel 10:4, 18-19. This vision was probably seen by Ezekiel on the fifth day of the sixth month of the sixth year of Zedekiah's reign (see Ezekiel 1:1-2 and 8:1), but we cannot be sure when God's presence actually left the temple. This story assumes that the vision was showing a process that began at the time when it was given and finished with the final destruction of Jerusalem.

on my behalf, while carefully avoiding touching anyone that he met and anything he came upon. Later, he told me that he had gone to Zedekiah's palace and made an appointment to see the king. Although he was not in the inner circle of the king's friends, he was known in the court and had been used for a few important missions since the time when he had been sent to Babylon with Elasah the son of Shaphan, carrying a report for King Nebuchadnezzar. Zedekiah called him into the throne room almost immediately and offered his condolences over the death of Azariah.

"Your brother served the nation well, Gemariah. He worked tirelessly for peace and unity for many years. In fact, he became High Priest before I was even born. It is unfortunate that your family has always had an internal conflict, but that only made his work all the more admirable."

"He did work hard to avoid conflict, O king. I know that it was not always easy, either, particularly when another member of the family seemed to be constantly working against it."

Incidentally, I suspect that Gemariah told me all of these details to remind me that my attitudes were not appreciated by anybody. But I already realised that – had I not been in prison for months for that very reason?

"Jeremiah does make it hard for all of us to do our jobs, sometimes," replied Zedekiah. "His attitudes have had a negative impact on the nation in many ways. But we haven't heard from him lately. Does Yahweh no longer speak with him? I would like to know if there is any more news from Yahweh."

"It is actually Jeremiah that I have come to speak to you about, my lord. You have not heard from him because he is in prison. Did you not know it, my lord?"

"In prison?" answered Zedekiah. He looked across questioningly at his friends who were seated nearby, listening to the conversation. Jehucal was among them and caught the king's eye.

"Yes, my lord," he said confidently, "Jeremiah was imprisoned in the house of Jonathan for trying to defect to the Chaldeans."

"Actually, since the Chaldean army had left Jerusalem to deal with the Egyptian army, Jeremiah was going to Anathoth to examine some land and sign the inheritance papers," said Gemariah.

"That's what he claimed," agreed Jehucal, "but many of us didn't believe a word of it. No land in Anathoth would have been worth anything at that time, any more than it would be now with the Chaldeans in the land. It was clearly nonsense."

"You could have asked me, Jehucal," said Gemariah. "What you call 'a story' was *true*."

"That may be, but it doesn't change the fact that he is constantly speaking against this city, and against the nation. It's no wonder many of us were suspicious."

Zedekiah was looking uncertainly from Jehucal to Gemariah and back again. "So where is Jeremiah now?" he asked.

"My lord, O king," said Gemariah, "Jeremiah has been locked up in a dungeon ever since. He is very sick."

Zedekiah was always a little sympathetic towards me. He wanted to hear messages from Yahweh, although he could never bring himself to obey any of God's commands through me – to him, the commands God gave were always too difficult.

"Jehucal, I want to see Jeremiah now," said Zedekiah. "I want to hear if he has any news from Yahweh."

When Kallai and Vaniah entered my cell again, my condition was quite different from when they had come to get me earlier in the day. Instead of wishing that they would just go away and leave me alone, I was pleased to see them and eager to follow – expecting to be led to King Zedekiah. God's voice had left its mark, as usual. I must be doing, not just sitting! Yahweh had given me a message for the king, so I expected to be called to see him, and I was not disappointed.

Kallai grudgingly told me that I was wanted at the palace and directed Vaniah to take me there.

I was still far from well, but walking was not the struggle it had been in the morning. As I walked across the courtyard in front of the palace, we saw Gemariah descending the steps from the palace.

"Jeremiah," he called, and there was more friendliness in his voice than I had heard from him for several years. He approached and looked me up and down. "You almost look like a new man. The king will wonder what I was talking about. Never mind, he wants to hear any messages you have from Yahweh, so don't keep him waiting. And, Jeremiah," – pleadingly – "why not let him hear a little bit of what he wants to hear? He'll be more likely to let you out of prison, you know."

I knew alright; but God's word was what it was – I couldn't change that.

"Thank you for speaking to him on my behalf, Gemariah, but surely you don't expect me to water down God's word?"

Gemariah sighed and said, "I suppose I knew that you wouldn't, but maybe sometimes it is better to be practical."

"Excuse me, sir," said Vaniah, "but I must take Jeremiah to the king immediately."

We entered the palace and were soon called in to see Zedekiah.

As we walked into the throne room, I was surprised to see that the room was empty, except for the king.

"Jeremiah," he said, "you aren't looking as bad as I expected, but you still don't look well, all the same." He turned to Vaniah and waved him away dismissively, saying, "Wait outside. I wish to speak to Jeremiah alone."[2]

Once the guard had left, Zedekiah asked if there was any news from Yahweh.

"Yes, God has given me a message for you, O king," I answered:

> " 'You shall be delivered
> into the hand of the king of Babylon.' "[3]

Zedekiah had been looking at me in eager anticipation, but when I said this, he pursed his lips and looked annoyed. Yahweh never did give him the messages he wanted to hear.

"But that's just what he said a while ago,"[4] complained Zedekiah.

"Did you expect something different? If you want God to give you a different message, O king, you need to behave differently towards him."

"I tried, didn't I? Didn't I organise the freeing of the slaves?"

"You did, O king, and God was pleased with it. But then what happened?"

---

[2] Jeremiah 37:17
[3] Jeremiah 37:17
[4] Jeremiah 21:7

"Ah, yes, well, it wasn't a good ending,[5] but that wasn't my fault."

"You are the king."

Once again, a look of annoyance crossed Zedekiah's face, and he leaned back in his throne. "I may be king, but after all, a king is only a king. I don't control everybody's thoughts. You seem to blame me for everything that happens. What wrong have I done you? None of the other prophets expect so much of me."

"What wrong have I done to you or your servants or this people, that you have put me in prison? Where are your prophets who prophesied to you, saying, 'The king of Babylon will not come against you and against this land'? Now hear, please, O my lord the king: let my humble plea come before you and do not send me back to the house of Jonathan the secretary, lest I die there."[6]

"Very well, I will not send you back there. I could free you, but you persist in making prophecies against me. Why do you prophesy and say, 'Thus says the Lord: Behold, I am giving this city into the hand of the king of Babylon, and he shall capture it; Zedekiah king of Judah shall not escape out of the hand of the Chaldeans, but shall surely be given into the hand of the king of Babylon, and shall speak with him face to face and see him eye to eye. And he shall take Zedekiah to Babylon, and there he shall remain until I visit him, declares the Lord. Though you fight against the Chaldeans, you shall not succeed'?[7] No, I have decided what to do. You shall be kept in the court of the guard, here in my palace."[8]

---

5 See Volume 4 – The Darkness Deepens, Chapters 14 and 15.

6 Jeremiah 37:18-20

7 Jeremiah 32:3-5

8 Jeremiah 37:21; Jeremiah 32:2

Accordingly, it wasn't long before I was given a room in the court of the guard. It was a mixed blessing. On the positive side, it was more difficult for my enemies to do away with me secretly, and it was much more hospitable than my cell in the house of Jonathan had been. Also, people in the city could visit me, and I would be able to pass on God's messages to them if necessary. The food was more consistent: every day, I was given a loaf of bread. But I was unable to move about freely, and I still knew nothing about what had happened to my mother.

Chapter 2

There is a future

To me, the gradual exhausting of supplies in the city didn't matter much. I was imprisoned in the court of the guard and received my food regularly every day – it was reliable, if not particularly tasty or varied. But I was concerned for others in the city, especially my mother, so I was very pleased when, the day after I was moved to the court of the guard, she came to visit me.

It was delightful to see her after months of not even knowing if she was still alive or whether she was aware of the outcome of my failed attempt to visit Anathoth.

"Oh, Jeremiah, it's so good to see that you are alive," she said, and her voice sounded younger than her years. I had last seen her on the morning, months before, when I had set off to inspect my newly-inherited land in Anathoth but had never made it past the city gates. A guard at the gate had brought an unjust charge of desertion, and I had been left languishing in a secret prison for months. Despite her relatively youthful voice, she looked older than she had on that disastrous morning. She had now reached the great age of 85, and had already outlived her husband Hilkiah, my father, by more than 30 years. "I have been so worried about you, Jeremiah," she said.

"And I about you," I replied. "How are you feeling?"

"I feel old, Jeremiah, but God must still have work for me to do, so I keep going. Does God continue to warn you about the coming destruction of Jerusalem?"

"Yes, mother, he does. I expect that this will be the last siege of Jerusalem. When it ends, Jerusalem will be destroyed, and the temple with it."

"The temple as well? What a tragedy."

"Yes – but when the temple is used as a place for worshipping idols and God's laws are completely ignored, the wonder is really that God has been as patient with us as he has."

"I suppose you are right. If only King Josiah had survived. Maybe he could have continued to lead some to righteousness."

"That task was only ever possible for a very few."

"So much has been lost, and everything that remains will be lost when Nebu-chad-nezzar takes the city."

We continued our discussion for some time, but carefully avoided speaking of the death of Azariah my brother, or the parlous state of worship in the temple over which my father and brother had presided. Jerusalem was no longer the home of honest worship of Yahweh, but had become a haven for idol-worshippers and hypocrites who claimed to worship Yahweh, but really did whatever they wanted.

It turned out that when I had been locked up in prison and my mother had been left alone in my home, she had found that she could not look after it properly without me being there. Instead, she had moved to live with Gemariah and Abigail, leaving my house unoccupied.

Now, as she left to return to Gemariah's house, we each expressed the hope that we would see each other again soon, but neither of us knew what would happen in those terrible days.

෴

The tenth year of Zedekiah was passing and the army of the king of Babylon continued to besiege Jerusalem. I was still shut up in the court of the guard – in Zedekiah's palace.

Then one day a strange thing happened. It was strange because once again it involved land.

Yahweh spoke to me, and I was glad, because it had been some time since he had done so and I wondered whether he was angry with my rebellious attitude. He said:

> "Behold, Hanamel the son of Shallum your uncle
> will come to you and say,
> 'Buy my field that is at Anathoth,
> for the right of redemption by purchase is yours.' "[9]

He then followed up these words with detailed instructions as to what I was to do when Hanamel came.

I have never been able to get used to the idea that I know things that will happen before they happen. Short term or long term, it doesn't really matter – although it is the short term prophecies that feel strangest. I know *what* is going to happen, but generally not *when* it will happen, and so from day to day I am expecting the predicted things to happen while the people around me are not. This

---

[9] Jeremiah 32:7

particular piece of advance warning from God was also one of the sort which I do not feel I can talk to others about. When God gives me messages for the people, I must tell them, but I would feel that I was boasting if I told people about this sort of private message. So I told no-one and waited for Hanamel to arrive.

When he came, he was led into my room, and I greeted him, "The Lord be with you, Hanamel."

"The Lord bless you," he replied. "Jeremiah, I have an offer for you which is also a request."

"Oh?"

"Buy my field that is at Anathoth in the land of Benjamin, for the right of possession and redemption is yours; buy it for yourself."

"Do you need the money?"

"Yes. You know that I couldn't sell the land to anyone at the moment. Who would want land that they can't get to and has been occupied by the Chaldeans anyway? The land is worthless, but I need money. You know how expensive food is becoming. Without this money, I will starve."

I knew that this was God's plan – and it would be good to help Hanamel too. We had been quite close as children, although he was a little younger than I.

By that stage in my life, I was no longer rich as the rest of my family was, but I still had some money that I could use for this purpose – particularly as I did not have to purchase bread for myself while I was in the court of the guard.

"How much was the land worth?"

"17 shekels of silver."

"I can afford that, Hanamel. But we can't exactly go out and view the land, can we?" I added, laughing. Then I stopped laughing and said, "It was going out to see my land last year that landed me in prison, and they still won't let me out."

"Look, I really appreciate this, Jeremiah, and I'm sorry that I can't show you the land. You'll just have to trust me about its size and value."

"That's alright. Well, I'll need to get the money organised now."

Although I was not free to leave the court of the guard, I did have freedom of movement within the area, and it was quite a busy place for legal matters. Perhaps the lawyers felt a little safer having soldiers around when they were transacting high-value business. This wasn't high-value, but it still required witnesses and all the rest of it.

The whole process would have been much easier if I had been free to leave, but instead I had to ask Hanamel to go to my brother Gemariah and arrange for the money to be collected from my home.

While he was away, I spoke to Baruch, who was working on legal matters in the court of the guard as he often did. This was one of the major ways in which scribes earned a living, and he agreed to help me with my purchase.

When Hanamel returned he had a bag of money with him, as well as the deed relating to the land. I quickly weighed out the money to make sure everything was ready, then I got some witnesses and we opened the sealed copy and began our transaction. Again I weighed out the 17 shekels for Hanamel on scales in front of the witnesses and signed both copies of the deed. I tied up the sealed copy with string, and shaped some of the special clay that we use for seals tightly around the string, so that it could not be untied without breaking the seal. Then I pressed my signet ring firmly into the clay and showed the witnesses the final result. They inspected the sealed deed and each man added his own seal to the sealed copy.

So I bought the field at Anathoth from Hanamel my cousin, and gave the deed of purchase to Baruch the son of Neriah son of Mahseiah, in the presence of Hanamel and the witnesses who had signed the deed of purchase, and in the presence of the Judeans who were sitting in the court of the guard.

This was really the most important part of the deal, because this was where God showed the lesson that the whole performance was intended to teach.

I charged Baruch in their presence, saying, "Thus says the Lord of hosts, the God of Israel: Take these deeds, both this sealed deed of purchase and this open deed, and put them in an earthenware vessel, that they may last for a long time. For thus says the Lord of hosts, the God of Israel: Houses and fields and vineyards shall again be bought in this land."[10]

The living prophecy was over, and I had done what God wanted me to do. But I still didn't understand why.

I returned to my room and prayed to Yahweh, saying: "Ah, Lord God! It is you who have made the heavens and the earth by your great power and by your outstretched arm! Nothing is too hard for you.

"You show steadfast love to thousands, but you repay the guilt of fathers to their children after them, O great and mighty God, whose name is the Lord of hosts, great in counsel and mighty in deed, whose eyes are open to all the ways of the children of man, rewarding each one according to his ways and according to the fruit of his deeds.

"You have shown signs and wonders in the land of Egypt, and to this day in Israel and among all mankind,

---

[10] Jeremiah 32:13-15

and have made a name for yourself, as at this day. You brought your people Israel out of the land of Egypt with signs and wonders, with a strong hand and outstretched arm, and with great terror. And you gave them this land, which you swore to their fathers to give them, a land flowing with milk and honey. And they entered and took possession of it. But they did not obey your voice or walk in your law. They did nothing of all you commanded them to do. Therefore you have made all this disaster come upon them.

"Behold, the siege mounds have come up to the city to take it, and because of sword and famine and pestilence the city is given into the hands of the Chaldeans who are fighting against it. What you spoke has come to pass, and behold, you see it. Yet you, O Lord God, have said to me, 'Buy the field for money and get witnesses' – though the city is given into the hands of the Chaldeans."[11]

Throughout my work as a prophet, there have only been a few times when God has answered my questions immediately and directly. But this was one such occasion, and his answer came straight away:

> "Behold, I am the Lord,
> the God of all flesh.
> Is anything too hard for me?
> Therefore, thus says the Lord:
> Behold, I am giving this city
> into the hands of the Chaldeans
> and into the hand of Nebuchadnezzar
> king of Babylon,
> and he shall capture it.
> The Chaldeans who are fighting against this city
> shall come and set this city on fire and burn it,
> with the houses on whose roofs
> offerings have been made to Baal

---

[11] Jeremiah 32:17-25

> and drink offerings have been poured out
> to other gods,
> to provoke me to anger.
> For the children of Israel
> and the children of Judah
> have done nothing but evil in my sight
> from their youth."[12]

Then the voice stopped, and for a while I thought the answer was over – though my question wasn't really answered. But God had certainly confirmed my expectations of the fate of my city, giving me confidence that this really was the end for Jerusalem. He was also confirming what he had already explained to me many times, that the punishment was coming because of faithlessness and disobedience. Had we ever done anything that was good, I thought? God gave me the answer to that question also:

> "The children of Israel have done nothing
> but provoke me to anger
> by the work of their hands, declares the Lord.
> This city has aroused my anger and wrath,
> from the day it was built to this day,
> so that I will remove it from my sight
> because of all the evil of the children of Israel
> and the children of Judah
> that they did to provoke me to anger
> – their kings and their officials,
> their priests and their prophets,
> the men of Judah and the inhabitants of Jerusalem."[13]

Again, a pause, and I had the opportunity to consider just how tragic God's words were. Jerusalem was the city in which he had chosen to put his name, yet his summary was that all it had ever done was to arouse his wrath.

---

[12] Jeremiah 32:27-30
[13] Jeremiah 32:30-32

Every possible group of people within the nation had angered him. Yet I couldn't help thinking, had not the inhabitants of the city turned to God in the time of Josiah's reformation?

> "They have turned to me their back
> and not their face.
> And though I have taught them persistently,
> they have not listened to receive instruction.
> They set up their abominations
> in the house that is called by my name,
> to defile it.
> They built the high places of Baal
> in the Valley of the Son of Hinnom,
> to offer up their sons and daughters to Molech,
> though I did not command them,
> nor did it enter into my mind,
> that they should do this abomination,
> to cause Judah to sin."[14]

What hope for the future could there be with a history and a present like that? Surely a final end must be coming quickly! But God's words continued, and the anger was fading:

> "Now therefore thus says the Lord,
> the God of Israel,
> concerning this city of which you say,
> 'It is given into the hand of the king of Babylon
> by sword, by famine, and by pestilence':
> Behold, I will gather them
> from all the countries to which I drove them
> in my anger and my wrath
> and in great indignation.
> I will bring them back to this place,
> and I will make them dwell in safety."[15]

---

[14] Jeremiah 32:33-35
[15] Jeremiah 32:36-37

The tempo had changed. The anger was gone and the long-suffering patience of God showed in every line. He told me how, in the end, my people would truly be his people and that they would have one heart and one way, to fear God forever. Despite our endless litany of failure, he would do good to us and bring us back after the impending exile. Then at last the final answer to my question came, with all of his earlier words forming a framework to support the answer. It was only with this background that I could really understand the answer to my question. God said:

"For thus says the Lord:
Just as I have brought all this great disaster
upon this people,
so I will bring upon them
all the good that I promise them.
Fields shall be bought in this land
of which you are saying,
'It is a desolation, without man or beast;
it is given into the hand of the Chaldeans.'
Fields shall be bought for money,
and deeds shall be signed and sealed and witnessed,
in the land of Benjamin,
in the places about Jerusalem,
and in the cities of Judah,
in the cities of the hill country,
in the cities of the Shephelah,
and in the cities of the Negeb;
for I will restore their fortunes,
declares the Lord."[16]

My enacted prophecy showed a hope for the future that I had not been able to see. I had concentrated on the coming destruction and exile, not the forgiveness and regathering.

---

[16] Jeremiah 32:42-44

God's plans for Judah and Israel were plans for good. Plans with hope.

ॐ

June, 587 BC – the 11th year of King Zedekiah

I have already mentioned that Zedekiah was not one to give up on asking for information from God – despite the fact that most of the time he then refused to listen to the words he received.

While I was still in the court of the guard, King Zedekiah sent Zephaniah the priest to me once more, this time with Pashhur the son of Malchiah. On the previous occasion it had been Jehucal – a grandson of the false prophet Hananiah – who had later done his best to kill me quietly by locking me up in the house of Jonathan.

Again, God had already prepared me for this, and I knew just what to say when they passed on the king's request.

As I opened the door to them, Zephaniah again looked ill at ease – forced to visit me, the worst trouble-maker of all priests.

"Greetings," I said, looking from one to the other, wondering which one of them would ask the question. "I was expecting you."

"Greetings to you, Jeremiah," replied Zephaniah, looking nonplussed for a moment, but then getting straight to the point. "The king says, 'Inquire of the Lord for us, for Nebuchadnezzar king of Babylon is making war against us. Perhaps the Lord will deal with us according to all his wonderful deeds and will make him withdraw from us.' "[17]

"I have three messages from God for you, which I

---

[17] Jeremiah 21:2

have written down in this scroll," I replied, handing them a scroll that I had written after God had told me what to say.[18] I hoped my writing was legible. "Firstly, thus you shall say to Zedekiah:

" 'Thus says the Lord, the God of Israel:
Behold, I will turn back the weapons of war
that are in your hands
and with which you are fighting
against the king of Babylon
and against the Chaldeans
who are besieging you outside the walls.
And I will bring them together
into the midst of this city.
I myself will fight against you
with outstretched hand and strong arm,
in anger and in fury and in great wrath.
And I will strike down
the inhabitants of this city,
both man and beast.
They shall die of a great pestilence.
Afterward, declares the Lord,
I will give Zedekiah king of Judah
and his servants and the people in this city
who survive the pestilence, sword, and famine
into the hand of Nebuchadnezzar king of Babylon
and into the hand of their enemies,
into the hand of those who seek their lives.
He shall strike them down
with the edge of the sword.
He shall not pity them or spare them
or have compassion.'[19]

---

[18] Note that there is no indication in the Bible that these messages were written in a scroll, but others were and the messages were meant to be reported to King Zedekiah, so it seems most likely.
[19] Jeremiah 21:4-7

"Secondly, to this people you shall say:

" 'Thus says the Lord:
Behold, I set before you the way of life
and the way of death.
He who stays in this city
shall die by the sword, by famine, and by pestilence,
but he who goes out and surrenders
to the Chaldeans who are besieging you
shall live and shall have his life as a prize of war.
For I have set my face against this city
for harm and not for good,
declares the Lord:
it shall be given into the hand
of the king of Babylon,
and he shall burn it with fire.'[20]

"And finally, to the house of the king of Judah say,

" 'Hear the word of the Lord,
O house of David!
Thus says the Lord:
"Execute justice in the morning,
and deliver from the hand of the oppressor
him who has been robbed,
lest my wrath go forth like fire,
and burn with none to quench it,
because of your evil deeds." ' "[21]

I was pleased to have delivered the messages, but had little hope that any of the groups – Zedekiah, his family or the rest of the people – would listen to God's word. As it turned out, not only did they refuse to listen, but very soon afterwards, they made me suffer for being his messenger.

---

[20] Jeremiah 21:8-10
[21] Jeremiah 21:11-12

Chapter 3

More payback

Pashhur wasn't gone for very long.

He had left with Zephaniah the priest, but soon returned with some of my worst enemies,[22] and wearing a vindictive look on his face.

He wasn't the ringleader – that was Shephatiah, the son of Mattan – but he was definitely a willing accomplice. So was Jehucal, the grandson of the false prophet Hananiah,[23] and the man behind my long incarceration in the house of Jonathan. Gedaliah, the son of Pashhur,[24] was in on it too, and they had the full authority of the king.

---

[22] Jeremiah 38:1

[23] See Jeremiah 37:3, 37:13 and 38:1

[24] The man Gedaliah is only mentioned once (in Jeremiah 38:1) and his father is probably not the same Pashhur as Pashhur the son of Malchiah mentioned above.

It's hard to say much that is positive about Zedekiah as a king. He was a weak ruler from the start and he never got any better. His friends ruled the roost and he did what they told him to do – except that he did have some boundaries he wouldn't let them cross. Not directly, at least.

I was sitting at the reading bench against the wall of my room in the court of the guard, reading a scroll of Isaiah and praying that Zedekiah would listen to the words God had just given him, when suddenly the door was flung open.

"There is Jeremiah, the traitor!" said a voice.

I remember feeling the icy grip of fear tighten around my chest as I turned quickly to see Shephatiah and Jehucal already halfway across the room, rushing towards me. Gedaliah the son of Pashhur and Pashhur the son of Malchiah were close behind.

"He should die for his treason!" shouted Jehucal.

I tried to stand, but I had barely started moving when Shephatiah grabbed me by the collar and yanked me backwards off the stool on which I had been sitting. As I fell I remember thinking that this was the end – these men intended to kill me.

My head hit the floor hard, and for some time I didn't really know what was going on, lying there helplessly as they ranted at me.

"How can we defend the city when people like you are telling everyone it is hopeless?" asked Shephatiah.

"Anyone who tells people to desert to the Chaldeans is fighting for the Chaldeans," said Pashhur.

"I say we should kill them," said Gedaliah.

"And that means we should kill *you*, Jeremiah," added Jehucal.

"You say that *we'll* all die by the sword, but it's you who ought to die," said Shephatiah.

There were many other complaints from them about what I had said in God's messages to the king, his household and the people. But after a while, I noticed that all of their comments were that I *should* die, not that they were actually going to kill me. I wasn't about to jump up and celebrate, but it looked as if my end probably wasn't coming immediately. However, I soon realised from their subsequent comments that, although they weren't planning to kill me directly, the plans they had would quickly lead to my death.

"We are going to put you into Prince Malchiah's[25] cistern," Pashhur informed me, with a cruel gleam in his eye.

"It doesn't have any water in it, so don't worry," said Gedaliah, laughing.

"And there probably aren't many rats, either," added Shephatiah.

"Of course," said Jehucal, "you probably know that the last loaves of bread in the city have been used up today."

"And the king has ordered that you be fed with bread, hasn't he?" said Gedaliah.

"What a pity!" said Jehucal.

"Don't worry, we'll give you all the bread we can find," said Pashhur.

"Oh, yes," said Gedaliah, sarcastically. "We must obey the king's commands, mustn't we?"

---

[25] This man was a son of King Zedekiah or possibly a man called Hammelech (a name which means "the king"). Note also that this Malchiah is a different man from the Malchiah who was the father of Pashhur.

By that time, I was able to speak again at last. "Did King Zedekiah tell you to do this?"

"More or less," said Shephatiah. "You know he hates you too."

"He said we can do whatever we want to do," said Jehucal. I later found that this was only partly true. If they'd been given complete freedom, they would have killed me immediately. Zedekiah had just enough strength of character and care for me to refuse them that opportunity.

"So why don't we go and do it now?" asked Gedaliah.

"Get up, old man," said Shephatiah, roughly.

I sat up slowly, rubbing the back of my head, and winced as I touched a large swelling and felt the stickiness of blood oozing onto my fingers.

"Oh look, he's hurt," sneered Jehucal.

"Of course he is, with the way you two have treated him," said Pashhur. "You didn't need to kick him, Jehucal." That explained the pain in my ribs. It must have happened while I was recovering from the crack on the back of my head.

"Pashhur, you're too soft with him. Everyone is – that's why he causes so much trouble," said Shephatiah. Then to me he said, "Get up now, traitor, or we'll have to drag you."

"And once we start, we won't stop until we drop you into the cistern – head first," said Jehucal threateningly.

Slowly I stood, with my hand pressed to the back of my head. Pashhur stepped closer, as if he would have liked to have helped me but didn't quite know how.

Jehucal grabbed my left arm and Shephatiah my right, and together they marched me out of the room and across to the stairs that led down into the lower levels of the palace. Gedaliah and Pashhur were following carrying torches, and with coils of rope hanging over their shoulders. The guards recognised my captors as the king's friends and accepted without question their explanation that the king had ordered them to put me into Malchiah's cistern, on the lowest level of the palace. Malchiah was the king's son and had supervised the building of the cistern into which I was to be thrown. Water collected in the courtyard was directed down below the palace into the cistern through channels and pipes. It had been a dry winter followed by a hot spring, and as we stumbled our way down the poorly lit steps, I hoped that Gedaliah was right that there was no water in it.

When we reached the bottom of the stairs, Gedaliah and Pashhur lit the torches they were carrying. As they flared, the flickering light revealed shadowy shapes scurrying across the floor and along the channels that directed water into Malchiah's cistern. Quickly, and not gently, I was led across the floor to a dark hole.

"Jump in," said Shephatiah.

"No," I said.

"Why not?" asked Jehucal, with a harsh laugh. "There's no water in there." They seemed to delight in mocking me.

"Stop it, you two," said Pashhur. "You know that we brought the ropes for lowering him down, so let's get on with it."

"But he might be too heavy," said Jehucal.

"Yes, we might slip and drop him," agreed Shephatiah.

They were obviously trying to frighten me, and it was working all too well.

Pashhur removed the rope that was hanging over his shoulder and threw one end to Shephatiah, then held up his torch. The light shone down into the dark hole and I caught a glimpse far below, not of water, but of a dark, evil-looking mud. I wondered who had come up with this way of getting rid of me. And did they plan to start lowering me and then deliberately let go of the ropes?

Gedaliah did the same with his rope, and soon the two ropes were stretched across the hole with a man at each end.

I looked desperately around for any way of escape, but my persecutors always seemed to make sure that there were at least two of them between me and the steps leading up to the surface.

"Don't even think about it," warned Shephatiah. "If you try to run away, we really will throw you in without any ropes."

"And enjoy doing it," said Jehucal.

"You don't need to say that," said Pashhur.

"Oh, let's stop the endless talking and get him in there," said Shephatiah, angrily.

He forced me to sit down on the side of the hole between him and Jehucal, then took the rope he was holding and put it under my right arm. "Keep it there," he said. "Don't let it fall or you might fall too."

"Hold this one under your other arm," said Jehucal, passing it under my left arm as he spoke, "and don't drop it either."

"Slide slowly off the edge," said Gedaliah; "we'll keep the ropes tight and lower you down."

I held the ropes as instructed and tried to slide off the edge while the four of them stood up above me holding the ropes tight, ready to take the load. After a few tries, I at last worked up the courage to really slide off and found myself hanging just below the level of the floor in almost total darkness. The torches had been placed in holders on the walls and little of their light made it down into the cistern. I was lowered down gradually, unable to tell either how far I had come or how far I had to go. Finally, my sandals touched something, and soon my legs were sinking in a foul-smelling mud that seemed eager to swallow me whole. As they continued to lower me, I continued to sink, wondering all the time just how deep the mud was.

Did they know how deep the mud was? It was all very well to have no free water in the cistern, but if the mud was deep enough, they wouldn't need any water to drown me – the mud would do the job well enough.

I continued to sink until, with the mud up to my shoulders, my feet finally touched the bottom of the cistern.

The ropes went loose and Shephatiah said, "He's down at the bottom. Pashhur and Gedaliah, drop your ends of the ropes and we'll pull the ropes up."

What I assumed were two ends of the ropes fell down on me, but of course, I couldn't see them in the darkness.

"Get the ropes out from under your arms, Jeremiah," said Shephatiah, as he started to pull them up.

I couldn't do it quickly enough and the ropes quickly began to burn and cut into my armpits as they were tugged from above.

"Slow down," I cried out in pain.

"We're in a hurry, you old fool," said Shephatiah, savagely.

"It's cold down here, we want to get up into the sunlight," added Jehucal.

So they drew the ropes out of the pit, raising them as quickly as they could. I did my best to avoid the injury they were trying to inflict, but I wasn't very successful.

"Well, we're off," said Shephatiah, once the ropes had been hauled up and coiled.

"We'll leave you to think about all the people in the city whom you have been betraying with your coward's talk," said Jehucal. "And we won't be coming back to feed you."

"Sorry, Jeremiah," said Pashhur, "but there's no more bread in the city, and you are getting just what you deserve."

I could hear the sound of the torches being collected, then the light flickered and faded as they started up the stairs.

I was alone in the silence. The darkness was complete, and Jehucal was right – it was cold.

I tried to lean into the mud, but instead I began to sink under it. I wouldn't be able to lean or sit – all I could do was to stand or I would die, engulfed and drowned by the mud. Maybe death was not far away. I was already beginning to shiver, and in this cold I wouldn't last long. My head was pounding and my ribs were hurting too – the lowering by rope hadn't helped the pain inflicted by Jehucal's foot.

But hadn't God promised me…?

I pushed that thought away because I was no longer sure exactly what God had promised me. But the thoughts kept coming back: had I truly been given a guarantee of survival? After all, everyone has to die eventually. Or had I just been given a promise that they could not overcome me for as long as God intended me to survive?

Time passed – it always does – but I had no way of telling how much time was passing. There was nothing to do except to pray and continue to stand. I tried moving across to the wall of the cistern but found that it didn't work very well because the floor sloped upwards quite steeply. It began to take me up out of the mud, but became too slippery to hold me up and I slid back down into the mud. As I slipped, though, my foot knocked against a raised section of the floor of the cistern. Maybe it was harder rock that had proved too hard to excavate. I suppose that the reason doesn't really matter – what mattered was that when I stood on that raised area, the mud was only a bit more than waist deep. In relief and hope, I tried to sit down, but it was still too deep. The only advantage was that I was slightly warmer not being completely surrounded by unpleasantly cold mud, though it still caked my upper body. But the truth was that my case was still completely hopeless. How could I rest or sleep when I couldn't even sit down?

What was I waiting for? Shouldn't I just give up and die? If I just sat down, the mud would take away all the trouble that my life had become. After all, I was nothing but trouble to everybody and nobody cared about me.

However, I have said it before, and it was true on this occasion too: I didn't quite know how to give up. God had not said that my work was finished, and anyway, what if the promise really was a promise? More than that, wasn't God's word a command? He had made me like an iron pillar and bronze walls, and had told me that I must not allow myself to be dismayed before them. Maybe it was his strength that was stopping me from giving up. If so, what was going to happen to save me?

෬

I didn't know it, but God had everything planned out, through a brave eunuch from Ethiopia. He was a servant of the king and I knew him a little. Why would a foreigner listen to Yahweh more than the people of Judah would? Yet he did, and God used his courage to save my life.

As I struggled just to survive through that endless night, coming closer and closer to exhaustion and death, God was working for my salvation.

Later on, Ebed-melech – his name just means "the king's servant", that's how unimportant he is – told me what he did when he heard the news about me being thrown into the cistern. It's an amazing story and his courage was amazing too. I got him to write it down in his own words, since I don't really remember much of what happened when he came to rescue me – I was too exhausted.

℃℞

Ebed-melech's story

It wasn't until the day after it happened that I heard how Jeremiah had been dumped into Prince Malchiah's cistern. I was furious, but what could I do? Logic told me I couldn't do anything, but my mind kept insisting that I had to try. I tried to get out of it, but after lots of arguing inside, I was finally convinced that I didn't have any choice. I was walking up towards King Zedekiah's throne room when I met one of his guards. He's a bit of a friend of mine, Jehonathan is, and I asked him if I could speak to King Zedekiah. I confess that, by that time, I was starting to get cold feet. After all, complaining to a king about his friends is a dangerous game to play, but my mind kept insisting.

You may be wondering whether it's really that easy to get to see the king, and, to be honest, it normally isn't. But my friend was on his way to deliver a message to King Zedekiah and he told me to come along. At the time, Zedekiah was actually in the area near the Benjamin Gate of the city, hearing some legal cases or something. On the way there, I explained my mission to Jehonathan and he stopped in mid-step and looked at me long and hard.

"Are you mad?" he asked, quietly. "Being a champion of Jeremiah is not the way to fame at the moment."

"I know," I said, "but I can't just let them get away with it, can I? I like Jeremiah and he really does seem to tell the truth from Yahweh. And I don't like seeing these young upstarts picking on a man of God who's twice their age."

"Hmmm," he mused, as he tapped the rolled-up message against the shaft of his spear. "Hmmm. If Zedekiah is letting his friends persecute Jeremiah, I don't think he's likely to listen to a servant like you."

"I have to try – it's just not fair."

"Well, it's your funeral, I suppose," said Jehonathan, and we walked on. I wished he had chosen a different idiom; hoped he wasn't going to be right.

We walked on and joined the crowd, and I started to think exactly what I was going to say to the king. After a few minutes, the case finished – I think it was an accusation of stealing food – and a man was dragged away in chains.

Then my friend, Jehonathan, moved towards the king, holding up his message, and I followed close at his heels. He handed over the message to the king, who started to open it, but then paused and looked enquiringly at me. My dark skin tends to attract attention here in Jerusalem – there aren't many of us Ethiopians around.

"He wants to talk to you about Jeremiah," said Jehonathan.

The king started and looked around him quickly. A guard standing nearby had also reacted and was looking interested.

"Irijah," said Zedekiah, beckoning, "go and make sure that the prisoner for the next case is ready."

Irijah moved away towards the guard-room of the gate and Zedekiah seemed to relax a little. "What do you want?" he asked me.

While standing in the crowd, I had worked out a fine-sounding speech that would convince King Zedekiah to free Jeremiah, but standing there before the king, I couldn't remember any of those beautiful words at all. "My lord, Shephatiah, Gedaliah, Jucal[26] and Pashhur have done evil in throwing Jeremiah into Malchiah's cistern. He'll die of hunger down there in the mud. There's no bread left in the city, and sure as eggs is eggs, *they* won't be lowering down any bowls of soup for him."

Zedekiah looked around again, but there was no-one nearby listening. It's amazing how sometimes you can be almost alone in a crowd. "So that was what they planned," he said, drumming with the fingers of his right hand on his knee, and not looking very pleased. He leaned forward and said to me quietly, "You're Ebed-melech, aren't you?"

I nodded, amazed that he knew my name. King Zedekiah is really quite a nice person if you keep him away from his friends... but a man chooses his friends.

"I think you are right," he continued. "I thought they would just lock him up, but I should have known better. Alright, take three men[27] – Jehonathan here can get another couple of men to help you; then get Jeremiah out of the cistern as quickly as you can. Preferably before my friends hear anything about it." He looked over his shoulder and saw Irijah returning with an unhappy-looking prisoner. "Go now," he said urgently, "and, Jehonathan, choose your helpers carefully. Don't tell anyone else what is happening until you have Jeremiah safe. Give him a room in a quiet area of the court of the guard – out of the dungeons."

By this time, Irijah was almost upon us, and Zedekiah

---

[26] Jucal is a variant of the name Jehucal.

[27] Note that this story uses the number three to match the ESV (2001). Apparently one Hebrew manuscript says three. Most translations – including the ESV (2011) – use thirty and the larger number may reflect the need to discourage the officials who had placed Jeremiah in the cistern from causing trouble.

looked at us almost apologetically before turning back to him and starting to discuss the next case. Irijah was looking at us curiously, but it was a curiosity tinged with anger, as if he somehow guessed what we were doing and didn't like it.

Jehonathan and I turned and walked towards the palace, and on the way, I asked him, "Who is Irijah, and why is he so interested in Jeremiah?"

"Irijah is a bitter enemy of Jeremiah's," said Jehonathan, "and he would be rejoicing if he knew where Jeremiah is at the moment. Maybe he does. He's always carrying on about trying to get Jeremiah."

"Why does he hate Jeremiah?" I asked. Here was yet another enemy I could be making.

"Irijah's grandfather, Hananiah, was a prophet," Jehonathan answered. "A false prophet. A few years ago, he contradicted Jeremiah's prophecies and said that the king of Babylon would be defeated and that all of the treasures taken from the temple would be brought back to Jerusalem within two years. It never happened, of course, but that wasn't the main point. A week or two later, Jeremiah said that he had been given a message from God saying that Hananiah had been telling lies while claiming they were prophecies from God. He said that Hananiah would die before the end of the year. And get this," Jehonathan stopped and grabbed my arm; "Hananiah was dead within weeks." He let go of my arm and we walked on as he continued, "Irijah blames Jeremiah. Funny really, because he keeps saying that Jeremiah is telling lies. Now I would have thought that if he didn't believe Jeremiah, he wouldn't believe he had the power to kill his grandfather either. Anyway, that's Irijah for you. Just a year or so ago, he managed to get Jeremiah beaten and locked up for a while,[28] but the king freed him that

---

[28] Jeremiah 37:13-15

time, too. If you want my advice, I'd say watch out for Irijah and his friends. And Shephatiah and his friends too," he added dryly.

By this time, we were back at the palace, and Jehonathan went to the barracks where the king's guards live to fetch another couple of men to help, while I went to the storehouse where all the unused items from the palace are stored. I fetched some old rags and worn-out clothes from there, as well as some ropes, then I went downstairs towards the lowest levels of the palace, the parts that were used as a prison. When I came to the deepest, darkest level, I found Jehonathan already there with a couple of his friends. I was glad that they had thought to bring torches, because without them we wouldn't have seen much. Even so, it was almost as if the darkness was swallowing up the fitful light of the torches, and the gaping hole in the floor seemed to ooze blackness.

A shallow gutter ran across the floor to the lip of the hole, with a few stones lying across it here and there, part of trying to keep rubbish out of the cistern, I guess. Beside one of the stones I saw what looked like a dead, desiccated rat, but it was hard to tell in the gloom. I didn't look too carefully. If these were the sorts of things flowing down towards the cistern, I wondered what items had got past the stones and were down there in the cistern with Jeremiah. More than just mud, I was sure. Again, I felt sorry for Jeremiah in his predicament, and angry with the men who continued to persecute him.

"Jeremiah!" I called, leaning over the dark opening and straining to see anything in the inky depths. I couldn't see anything at all, so I was rather glad when I heard his response:

"Is that you, Ebed-melech? Oh, thank Yahweh! I never thought to hear anyone's voice again. I had given up hope." His muffled voice sounded tired and there was none of the hope that normally enlivened his voice.

"You're not going to die this time, Jeremiah," I replied. "The king has sent us to get you out of there."

"How long have I been in here? It's so dark in here, I can't see whether it is day or night," he croaked. "What time is it?"

"It's the middle of the afternoon and as far as I can tell, you have been in there since yesterday morning. So let's get you out of there quickly."

I took one of the ropes and gave it to Jehonathan. "You take this rope with one of your friends and lower it down to Jeremiah."

One of the men looked a little doubtful in the flickering torchlight. "Is that really Jeremiah, the son of Hilkiah, down there?" he asked, and he looked at Jehonathan accusingly. "You never told me we were going to help him. He's a traitor, isn't he?"

"No, he's not," answered Jehonathan. "You can't believe everything you're told, you know. Who said he was a traitor?"

"Well, it was Pashhur and Irijah," the man replied. "They said he is encouraging people to betray us to the Babylonians."

"No he isn't," I said. "Jeremiah is just telling people that God says we are going to lose this war anyway and that if we give in quietly, we will be treated well, but if we keep fighting we will still lose and everything will be worse for everyone. That's not being a traitor, that's trying to help."

"Yeah, well," said the other, "I'm finding it a bit hard to tell the difference. We're in the army to fight, and he's telling everyone to give up. That doesn't sound very patriotic."

"He's been saying the same sorts of things for a long time now, you know. And he gets things right, too. He said the Babylonians would come, and they did. Forty years ago he started saying they would come, and at the start, everyone laughed at him because no one could imagine Pharaoh letting Babylon run wild in his neck of the woods, but then Nebuchadnezzar came along and people stopped laughing. Then just a couple of years ago when the army of Pharaoh started to advance towards us, Nebuchadnezzar took his army away from our walls for a while. Everyone yelled and cheered and rejoiced, but Jeremiah said Nebuchadnezzar would come back with his army, and he was right again. And what about Irijah's grandfather, too? Look, if God says that Nebuchadnezzar is going to conquer Jerusalem, surely it's pretty stupid to keep fighting – but that's what your bosses want you to do. If they would just give in as Jeremiah says, lots more of you soldiers would stay alive."

It was a long speech. I don't normally talk very much, but sometimes things need to be said. Our leaders – even King Zedekiah – are all too concerned about their own skins and don't seem to care about anyone else's. Anyway, in this case the speech managed to convince Jehonathan's friends enough that they helped us lower the ropes down to Jeremiah. By that time, my eyes had got more used to the darkness and I could see that he was up to his waist in wet, slimy mud. We dropped down some old clothes to him, and at my insistence, he put some of them between his arms and the ropes – I had a suspicion that the mud would not want to let him go, and that we would have to pull pretty hard to lift him out. And so it proved. It wasn't thin, runny mud; nor was it thick, firm earth; it was mud into which you would pretty quickly sink, and then you'd be stuck there. We started to lift him, but soon realised that meant trying to lift all the mud out of the bottom of the cistern as well.

We pulled, and we pulled, but we weren't getting far, and it was clear that the ropes were cutting into Jeremiah quite badly. After a while, Jehonathan told Jeremiah to kick his legs around, and that did the trick. With various sucking and slurping noises, the mud finally let him go and he was left dangling in mid-air with bits of mud falling off him.

When we got him up to floor level, he really looked a mess: covered with mud from head to foot and looking utterly exhausted. I'm not sure how much longer he would have lasted in that cistern if we hadn't come when we did. You can't get much sleep when you're waist-deep in slimy mud that will drown you if you don't keep your head up. And he was cold, too: he was shivering and shaking when we finally helped him up over the edge so that he could collapse on the floor.

Poor Jeremiah. We took him out of those gloomy depths and led him up to ground level where we helped him to clean himself up a bit. I insisted that he eat my lunch – there's precious little of any sort of food left in the city, so he wouldn't have got anything otherwise. Then, as the king had commanded us, we put Jeremiah into a room where he would feel safe and could recover from his ordeal.

You know, God expects a lot from his servants, particularly when it involves trying to warn others and save their lives. Yahweh cares, and he wants his worshippers to care too. I must admit though, I find it hard to care for people like Shephatiah, Gedaliah, Jucal and Pashhur.

So God did protect Jeremiah after all, but it's a bit funny that he should have done so through me – a foreigner, and a slave – when there are so many members of his chosen people who could have done the job. Maybe that is one of the reasons why Jerusalem is to be destroyed....

Chapter 4

Who's ruling anyway?

I recognised the palace of the kings of Judah instantly, but the uniforms of the soldiers that surrounded it were Chaldean.

Beside the ruins of the guardhouse and the gates of the courtyard, other men were sitting, relaxed and happy, attended by servants in splendid livery, who plied them with food and drink. Their fine clothing announced them to be important officials, while their hairstyle and the ornaments on their heads showed that they, too, were Chaldean.

Scores of Chaldean soldiers in their distinctive red uniforms stood guard at the entrances to the palace, weapons at the ready.

Suddenly, four soldiers appeared in the main doorway, each leading – or dragging – a woman. Another five soldiers followed, swords in hand.

As the women descended the steps I heard their words, and with the uncanny certainty that comes in visions and dreams, I knew that they were speaking of Zedekiah:

> "Your trusted friends have deceived you
> and prevailed against you;
> now that your feet are sunk in the mud,
> they turn away from you."[29]

Zedekiah's friends had left me to sink in the mud, and now they had apparently done the same with Zedekiah, whether literally or figuratively. I didn't know in what way they had abandoned him to look after themselves, but it was no surprise to know that they had.

As I continued to watch, more women and girls were led out of the palace and collected together in a group at the bottom of the stairs. I recognised some of them as wives and daughters of the king.

They were clearly terrified as they stood there, surrounded by soldiers who were waiting for further orders but not afraid to make comments while they waited. Fortunately for the women, none of them understood Aramaic, or their terror would have been still greater.

Some boys were also being led out. I recognised none of them, but nevertheless understood that they were the sons of King Zedekiah.

But where was the king himself, I wondered? The scene I was watching must be occurring in the aftermath of the current siege: the defeat of Jerusalem. Had Zedekiah been killed? No, God had said that he would be taken away to Babylon as a captive. Had he already been taken away at this point?

---

[29] Jeremiah 38:22

At last an order was given and the women were led towards the officials seated in the courtyard. I watched as they were presented to the officials one by one.

The first was welcomed with mocking and ridicule, but she was brave and met it all with a quiet stoicism. After the officials had sneered at the army of Judah and the absence of protection they had offered to their womenfolk, she replied, "At least our king has escaped."

"Oh, you think he's escaped, do you? Let me straighten you out. Your brave and self-sacrificing king who ran away by night and left all of you to look after yourselves has been caught."

The woman looked aghast, and that was the end of her stoicism. The officials enjoyed her discomfiture and I was glad when the vision ended so that I did not have to see the conclusion of the unpleasant scene.

❦

Following my rescue from the cistern by brave Ebed-melech, I had been taken to a different room in the court of the guard. Zedekiah had probably intended to hide me from my persecutors for a while; if so, it worked.

I had had two days to recover a little when the king called me to a secret meeting. Zedekiah's friends made most of the decisions in the kingdom, but he wasn't altogether happy with that. They didn't care about Yahweh at all, but Zedekiah did to some extent, so he called me to a room at the third entrance of the house of God.

Imagine that – a king who has to organise a meeting outside his palace just to stop his friends from interfering! If a king can't run his own palace, what hope has he of running a kingdom?

Anyway, I was taken from my room and led quickly

by a guard through the king's special entrance to the temple. I wasn't told why I was being taken there, and I must admit, I was rather worried that it might be another attempt to kill me. However, it turned out that Zedekiah had chosen it as the safest place to meet, since he didn't want his friends around. None of them were frequent visitors to the temple!

I was led into one of the side rooms in the entrance area and was surprised to see Zedekiah sitting there alone. No guards or advisors were present – it was just him and me.

He waited until the guard had walked out and shut the door before saying, without preamble, "I will ask you a question; hide nothing from me."

Well, I'm afraid I wasn't very eager to do what he asked. Giving Zedekiah detailed answers had got me into a lot of trouble in the recent past, and I hadn't forgotten it.

At that time I was really losing my way a bit. I still wanted to pass on God's messages, but I was no longer taking the stand I should have been taking. An iron pillar doesn't negotiate for its safety, but that's what I started to do.

"If I tell you, will you not surely put me to death?" I asked, cautiously. "And if I give you counsel, you will not listen to me."

When I look back at it, it is clear that I was giving way to fear. It all seemed quite reasonable, but it wasn't presenting myself as the immovable object that God had told me to be. I regret that, and am very thankful to God for being patient with me. You see, I already knew what I had to say to Zedekiah: God had told me and shown me, but I had let my suffering become more important to me than delivering Yahweh's messages. I was afraid.

King Zedekiah gave me the guarantee I craved. "As the Lord lives, who gave us life, I will not put you to death or deliver you into the hand of these men who seek your life."

I knew I wouldn't be able to get any better assurance from him than that, so I began to tell him God's message:

"Thus says the Lord, the God of hosts,
the God of Israel:
If you will surrender
to the officials of the king of Babylon,
then your life shall be spared,
and this city shall not be burned with fire,
and you and your house shall live.
But if you do not surrender
to the officials of the king of Babylon,
then this city shall be given into the hand of the
Chaldeans,
and they shall burn it with fire,
and you shall not escape from their hand."[30]

"I am afraid of the Judeans who have deserted to the Chaldeans," countered Zedekiah, "lest I be handed over to them and they deal cruelly with me."

"You shall not be given to them. Obey now the voice of the Lord in what I say to you, and it shall be well with you, and your life shall be spared. But if you refuse to surrender, this is the vision which the Lord has shown to me: Behold, all the women left in the house of the king of Judah were being led out to the officials of the king of Babylon and were saying,

" 'Your trusted friends have deceived you
and prevailed against you;
now that your feet are sunk in the mud,
they turn away from you.' "[31]

I then told him the rest of my vision, warning him

---

[30] Jeremiah 38:17-18
[31] Jeremiah 38:22

that he himself would be seized by the king of Babylon and the city burned with fire. If he gave in to his fears, the reality would be even worse than those fears.

"Let no one know of these words, and you shall not die," the king told me. "If the officials hear that I have spoken with you and come to you and ask what was said, then you shall say to them, 'I made a humble plea to the king that he would not send me back to the house of Jonathan to die there.'"

"I will do as you say, O king. And I will in fact make that humble plea to you: please do not send me back to the house of Jonathan or to any other prison. With no bread left in the city, prisoners will be left to die of hunger."

King Zedekiah told me that I would be returning to the court of the guard, and shortly afterwards I was led back to my room in the palace.

By this time there was little left to hope for in Jerusalem. There was no more bread and few other provisions remained. The only possibility was that somehow a miracle would cause the Chaldeans to leave their positions. Nothing else could save the city.

I don't know how the officials heard about my private discussion with King Zedekiah or how they managed to find out where I was, but a very short time later, they all crowded into my room and demanded to know what our discussion had been about. I answered as the king had instructed me, and they had to accept my word because the conversation had not been overheard.

CR

After my interview with King Zedekiah, events inside Jerusalem began to move quickly.

With the bread supply in the city exhausted, starvation and capitulation could not be far away.

I was still shut up in the court of the guard and could not see first-hand what was happening in the city, but I was told that many people were dying in the frequent attacks made on the city by Chaldean soldiers, as well as from the constant bombardment from their catapults. Disease was also spreading, as people – particularly the poor – became weaker from malnutrition.

Violence, too, was an ever-present danger, with men of violence being quick to seize any opportunity to steal precious food.

How much longer could the city endure?

Being trapped in a city under siege made it easy to concentrate on events in the city to the exclusion of everything else, but apparently, outside the city, the Chaldean army was still trying to clean up the last pockets of resistance in Judah.

Lachish and Azekah in the southwest had held out longer than any of the other fortified cities of Judah,[32] as had a few units of the army that had kept away from cities and continued to act independently in the open country.

This much I already knew about events elsewhere, but the day after my secret interview with King Zedekiah, I met an acquaintance from an earlier siege,[33]back when the body of Jehoiakim had lain rotting beside the road and Jeconiah his son had tried unsuccessfully to resist the might of the Chaldeans. At that time, this man had been a captain of the guard and had explained to me how a daring Judean counter-attack had repelled and damaged a Chaldean battering ram. Now, as I understood it, he was a more senior officer in the army and had just

---

[32] Jeremiah 34:7

[33] See Volume 4 – The Darkness Deepens, Chapter 3

returned from a long and dangerous assignment outside the city.

It is amazing what can be right under everyone's nose without anyone knowing about it! Most people in Jerusalem know about the water supply tunnel that was constructed in Hezekiah's time, but very few know of the other tunnels that make it possible for people to enter and leave Jerusalem without ever passing through the gates or climbing over the walls. Maybe if I had known about them on that freezing, wind-swept night back in the days when Jeconiah reigned, I might have found it easier to get into the city[34] – but then again, maybe I would have been killed by an over-zealous guard in the process!

Anyway, this man had been outside Jerusalem working as a guerrilla fighter for almost a year, striking the Chaldeans and other enemies whenever he could, as the leader of a small band of highly trained men. His gift for describing events made his adventures live in my mind. For him, there had often been enemies on every side, but he had survived all of the terrors and re-entered the city through one of these secret tunnels while I had been in Malchiah's cistern, struggling just to survive.

"The Chaldeans have concentrated their forces around the main cities of Judah, particularly Jerusalem, Lachish and Azekah," he told me, "but they haven't bothered much with other areas." He spat on the ground before continuing sarcastically, "So, can you guess what our charming neighbours have done?"

"I have no idea," I answered. I had spoken God's word against all of Judah's neighbours, but I knew that Judah was to suffer first.

"Well, Edom was the first to see the opportunity to redraw their borders so as to snatch a little bit of extra

---

[34] See Volume 4 – The Darkness Deepens, Chapter 1

land. Our land. Of course, they didn't push too far into Judah – that might have brought a confrontation with King Nebuchadnezzar. No, they just grabbed small chunks of extra land, strategic areas mostly – and some booty as well. Enough land to push their borders further away from their main cities. A bit more secure for them, I suppose." He spat again. "And enough booty to make it all worthwhile – including slaves. We did what we could, and so did the others, but what can a few small groups do against an army?

"Many of our people have just run away to hide in the countries around. I hope they survive, but I wish they had stayed to help the fight." He looked at me apologetically, "I know you've told us not to fight against the Chaldeans, sir, but it's an old habit for me. I can't stop it now."

I couldn't help wondering to myself how many people are ever willing to change their life at God's command.

"Anyway, Moab and Ammon saw what was happening and decided to join in too," he continued. "They came in and took more land and more booty. Even told us that they were coming, they did – laughed at us, really.[35] Then they brushed us aside as easily as you might push off a blanket, sir, and they took away more slaves, too. Our people who live in the countryside have faced threats on every side. Just as you said, sir. 'Terror on every side', wasn't it?"

I agreed sadly, and he continued to tell me tales of terror that filled me with fear for what was about to come upon Jerusalem. What would happen to my family? How would a victorious Chaldean army treat my mother? My brother Gemariah and his family were still in the city; so also were Azariah's son Seraiah, the High Priest, and his family; my cousin Hanamel and his family; and many,

---

[35] Hints are found in Jeremiah 48:25-27; 49:1-2 and Zephaniah 2:8-10.

many others. There were so many who were endangered by this siege, including people like Ebed-melech – but at least him I could pray for, since he was not one of my nation.

"You warned us, sir," said my informer, "you truly did. And now I'm back here in the city for which you've predicted utter destruction. Am I mad, sir?"

I couldn't help thinking that he was actually a very brave man, but, sadly, one who was more loyal to his king than to his God – a choice that will always prove costly.

Chapter 5

A little bit of hope

The last loaf of bread I ate in the besieged city was the one I had eaten on the morning that I was thrown into Malchiah's cistern – when my captors warned me the bread in the city had run out. By the time Ebed-melech freed me I was very hungry, not having eaten for more than a day. However, that relative freedom did not do much to ease my hunger, as being stuck in the court of the guard gave me no chance to search for food anywhere else.

Two days after my secret meeting with Zedekiah, there was no longer any food of any sort available for me in the court of the guard, and I slowly began to starve.

Talking to Lappidoth – the talkative soldier who was so good at telling stories – helped to pass the time, though, and gave me a chance to learn some of what had been going on outside Jerusalem.

"Did you know that there are still prophets in other parts of the country, giving people messages from God?" he asked me one morning as we sat together outside my room in the court of the guard.

"No, I didn't. Are they genuine? Are they truly prophets of God, or prophets who speak for themselves?"

"Oh, I wouldn't know, sir. I know that some of your prophecies have come true, but apart from that, I can't tell a good prophet from a bad one."

"Do they tell people to worship Yahweh? To repent? To prepare for coming destruction? Do they tell people to surrender to the Chaldeans?"

"Oh, no, sir!" he said, looking shocked by my last question. "These are *soldiers*, sir. Sorry, sir," he said, looking at me apologetically, "but these are not religious men like you, they are brave fighters who are willing to give their lives to defeat the Chaldeans."

"So people are either brave *or* religious, are they Lappidoth?"

"Ah, well, sir, I didn't quite mean that, sir," he said, awkwardly, looking down at his feet.

I put my hand on his shoulder and reassured him, "Don't worry, Lappidoth – I think I know what you mean, and I'm not offended."

"I've never really thought about prophets like you being brave, sir," he said, looking over at me again. "But now that I think about it, I'm not sure that I would find it very easy to stand up against my own nation as you have done, sir."

It was the first time during all my years as a prophet that anyone had ever suggested that being a genuine prophet might actually require courage, rather than the prophet being a coward who wouldn't fight. And he even extrapolated that logic to suggest that any prophet who speaks against his nation is probably more likely to be genuine than one who speaks words his nation will want to hear. It was interesting logic that seems to describe the history of prophets rather well.[36] Throughout history, God's prophets have always delivered messages of warning and condemnation, and many have died at the hands of a hostile nation.[37]

He looked at me with renewed respect and said, "I guess that they are all false prophets, sir. Put it this way, they all disagree with you, sir, and they all fight against the Chaldeans." He stopped, then said thoughtfully, "I suppose I do too. Hmm."

We continued to talk about his work outside Jerusalem as a leader of a group of guerrilla fighters, and soon he began to tell me another story.

"On one occasion," he said, "we had to carry instructions from Jerusalem to Lachish. A messenger came to us out of Jerusalem through the secret passages and gave us the message. That part was easy. But we knew that getting the message into Lachish wasn't going to be so easy, with thousands of Chaldeans camped all around the city."

"Are there any tunnels leading into Lachish?"

"None that we know of, sir."

"So what did you do?"

"First, we tried sneaking into their camp during the night, trying to get close enough to the walls to shoot an arrow – with the note tied to it – over the walls into the city. But that almost got us all caught, and two of my men were killed in the chase that followed."

---

[36] Jeremiah 28:7-9

[37] Matthew 5:11-12; Acts 7:52

His eyes held the intent story-telling look that I had seen in them before, so I didn't interrupt.

"We tried again the next night, but the Chaldeans had stepped up their watch, and that time we didn't even get near the camp itself before they spotted us. We had to run for our lives again. Imagine running as fast as you can on a moonless night, hearing shouts and footsteps close behind you all the while. Sometimes arrows whizzed past us, and sometimes we stopped, ready to fight off an attacker, only to find that it was one of our own men! It was terrifying."

He stopped and looked at me wryly as he noticed the word he had inadvertently used, evidently remembering God's frequent refrain of "terror on every side!"

"Anyway, we escaped alright," he continued, "but the message still wasn't delivered and we weren't going to try the same way again. It would have meant our deaths – no doubt about it. Now, you may not know it, but messages are often sent to people outside our cities using beacon fires from inside the city. We don't normally do it the other way, for obvious reasons, but we decided that we had to take the risk this time."

I wondered to myself what these obvious reasons were, but hoped that his further explanations would make it clear. They did.

"The next day we hunted for a place on a hill where we could light a fire that would be seen by the watchmen in Lachish but not by the Chaldeans. Imagine my unit hiding on the side of a hill with a smaller hill between us and the Chaldeans. We chose the place in daylight – and very carefully too – so that we could be sure that we could see the top of the wall of Lachish, but not the Chaldean army that surrounded it. A very fine line. Very risky. We knew that as soon as we lit the fire, we would be easy targets for any Chaldeans who saw it. We would have to build up the fire as quickly as possible, hurry to send the message using our special code and then hotfoot it out of there as quickly as we could. It's not something that we ever risk normally, but the message had to be delivered."

Now I understood the obvious reasons.

"We stayed hidden there for most of the day," said Lappidoth, "and none of the Chaldean units saw us. They were moving around there constantly, and we just hoped that they wouldn't stay camping anywhere nearby.

"As dusk settled, we collected all the wood we would need, and some leafy branches to make the signals with – you know, for hiding the flame periodically to spell out the message. Once it was completely dark and we had made sure that we couldn't see any of the Chaldean fires around the walls of Lachish, we lit our fire. We were all very much on edge as the fire built up, keeping a careful eye on the blackness surrounding us, as you might expect. We started sending the message as soon as we could, and then waited desperately for the confirmation when we finished. But the watchmen of Lachish obviously weren't used to receiving messages any more! Since there was no acknowledgement, we had to go through the whole message again, and of course, by that time we were all imagining shouts from all directions, and other fires too. All sorts of fears from all around.

"We made the fire even bigger before trying to send the message again – just to make doubly sure that they would be able to see the fire from Lachish. Soon after our man started signalling again, we really did start to hear some shouts, probably from the top of the hill that was between us and the Chaldean army. While they were that far away, we didn't have a problem, but as the branch was waved slowly up and down, we heard the shouts coming closer. The soldiers were obviously running down the hill opposite us and had nearly reached the valley. Soon they would be crossing the narrow valley and starting the climb towards us. The rest of us were ready for any attack from the darkness, facing away from the light to give us the best chance of seeing any possible danger.

"There were just a few more waves of the branch to go – I was keeping track by the sound – when the man with the branch suddenly gave a muffled shout." Lappidoth mimed the sudden glance over his shoulder as he said, "I turned around, like this, and saw him fall to the ground with an arrow in his back. I ran over quickly and grabbed the branch. I was fairly sure where he was in the message, so I just carried on from there. As I waved the branch down and up again, alternately covering the fire and letting its light be seen, I felt the horrible feeling of being completely unprotected, just waiting for an arrow to hit me in the back. Arrows were falling all around me and my men, but no-one else had been hit by the time I finished the message. I watched eagerly for a confirmation from the walls of Lachish. Had the message been received? But as I turned briefly to check the situation, I could see the dim shadows of many men running up the hill towards us.

"We never knew whether that message got through or not. I told my men to run for it and we all sprinted off up the hill behind our fire, escaping into the darkness. Unfortunately it was too late for three of my men who had been a short way down the hill, making sure that nobody could get to the fire without us knowing about it. It was hard to see in the dark, but I would guess that about twenty Chaldean soldiers attacked them – they didn't stand a chance. Fighting in the dark against an invisible enemy when a fire behind makes you a perfect silhouette… well, let's just say that they didn't have much hope.

"We lost six men trying to deliver that message, and after all that, we never knew whether we had delivered it successfully or not. After causing such a hullabaloo near

Lachish, we had to move on from there, travelling through the night so that we were far away by morning. In war, you can't always achieve what you want.

"Those six men were friends of mine. We had been through a lot together, and it really hit me hard to lose them like that. Then, only a week later, we heard that Lachish had fallen to the Chaldeans, so our message didn't help them anyway. Hundreds, maybe thousands died. The Chaldeans are vicious and cruel."

"You're right," I agreed. "In fact, another prophet of God a few years ago described them as 'a bitter and hasty people'.[38] If only people had surrendered instead of fighting."

"But who would do that?" Lappidoth asked. "Everyone has heard of the cruelty of the Chaldeans. Who would surrender to people like that when there is a chance – even if it's only a faint chance – that you might escape?"

"I can understand the dilemma," I said, "but if you just trust God, he will protect you. You could even have done it yourself."

"With all due respect, sir, why don't you?"

"One of the reasons why I have been locked up for almost two years now is to make sure that I *don't* go out to the Chaldeans."

"I suppose so," he said, thoughtfully. "Your job as a prophet has cost you a lot, sir, hasn't it?"

"Maybe, but your job will cost you even more, Lappidoth, if you don't follow God's instructions. Why won't you do it?"

"Oh, I couldn't do that, sir. I'm a soldier. I fight for my country, for my town, for my king. The priests still tell

---

[38] Habakkuk 1:6

me that Yahweh will save the temple, so I'm hoping that they are right."

"But Yahweh himself has told you that there will be terror on every side. The temple will not be saved. It will be burned with fire. Even this court of the guard and the palace of the king – all will be burned. And those who survive the pestilence that is already spreading through the city will be slaughtered by the Chaldeans."

"Well, I'll just have to take my chances, sir. I can't give up now."

CR

Thirst kills within days, but hunger takes weeks.

Water, such as it was, was still freely available in the city – even prisoners like me could have as much to drink as we wanted. But the water was not the cool, clear, refreshing liquid that I remember from my childhood in Anathoth: water that bubbled from a spring and trickled away down my favourite hillside. This water was a dirty brown liquid with an unpleasant smell and an even more unpleasant taste. When spilled on any material, this water left a brown stain. Everyone was afraid that it would make them sick, and maybe it did. Sickness was certainly rife in the city and many were dying – some in agony, others in overwhelming weakness.

After a week without food, I was not feeling very good. It wasn't that I felt particularly hungry – the worst of the hunger had passed by that time. It was more a feeling of tiredness, of lethargy and lassitude that filled me and made every task hard work.

Lappidoth, however, didn't seem to be suffering any of the effects of hunger that I was feeling, so I asked him about it. He looked surprised, then quickly stood up and hurried away. A few moments later, he returned with his right hand hidden in the folds of his uniform. He looked around to make sure that no-one could see what he was doing, then surreptitiously pulled out his hand and offered me a small cake of figs.

"Have this, sir."

I cautiously took it and held it under my cloak, looking at him questioningly.

"I didn't think about your food, sir," he said. "Knowing that you are from the high priest's family, I just assumed that you would be getting food on the black market like all of the other rich people."

"You mean rich people can still get food in the city even when there is no bread left?"

"I don't like to be rude, sir, but do you really need to ask? Money is the answer to everything, you know. Rich people can always get what they want." There was no reproach or anger in his voice. It was as if he considered the benefits of riches to be a reasonable rule of nature.

"Not if you have made enemies like I have," I said bitterly. "If you have, you get nothing. Nothing."

"Well, now you have something," he replied soothingly. "Eat it up while there's no-one around."

I followed his advice, and my first food for a week tasted delicious as I wolfed it down. Once I had finished it, I asked, "Where did that come from?"

"Oh, the king looks after his senior officers and the men in his special forces. No bread, of course – there really is none of that left in the city, however much you're willing to pay – but there are still limited amounts of other sorts of food, and people with money or influence get the first go at them. What do you expect? But it won't be long before those supplies run out too."

As he finished, I saw Ebed-melech walking across the courtyard towards us. "Now here comes a man who is both brave *and* religious," I said. "After the king's friends had thrown me into Malchiah's cistern, Ebed-melech went to King Zedekiah and told him that what his friends had done was evil."

"Really? That *is* brave!" He turned around and looked at Ebed-melech with respect as he approached.

"The Lord bless you, Ebed-melech," I called out.

"The Lord keep you, my lord Jeremiah," he replied.

"This is Lappidoth," I said, "a leader and a soldier in King Zedekiah's army."

"Ebed-melech?" said Lappidoth. " 'Servant of the king', eh? Yet Jeremiah has been telling me that you told the king that his friends were doing evil. That's a brave thing for anyone to do, let alone a servant of the king. Which friends were they?"

"Shephatiah the son of Mattan, Gedaliah the son of Pashhur, Jucal the son of Shelemiah, and Pashhur the son of Malchiah, sir," said Ebed-melech, a little glumly.

"Have they tried to pay you back yet?"

"No-o-o, not directly, but apparently they have been saying bad things about me to the king."

"They're dangerous men, you know. They won't forget."

"I know. I'm afraid of them."

"The Chaldeans might be worse though."

"I'm afraid of them, too." He turned to me and asked, "Is there any chance that God will relent, sir?"

"I don't think so," I said. He accepted the answer, but looked as if he had more to say. "Is that all," I asked, not wanting to sound as if I was trying to get rid of him.

"Yes, sir, ah… and sir," he looked awkward, "I wanted to check whether you had been given any food. I know that those terrible men still have food to eat, and I have been given a little, but I wondered if you had been given any, sir."

"Don't worry, Ebed-melech. Lappidoth here has just given me some," I reassured him.

"I'm glad to hear it. But I really must go, sir. I have work to do for the king."

He left quickly, and Lappidoth and I continued to talk for a while until he too had to leave.

No sooner had he left than the power of Yahweh rushed upon me. As usual, there was a feeling that I was being filled with light and heat from God, but somehow it was more gentle than usual. I heard the voice of God so clearly and loudly that I felt certain that anyone nearby must have heard it too. I looked around, but the few soldiers that I could see were paying no attention to me, and clearly had not heard the voice that rang with kind certainty.

Impelled by the words God had spoken, I stood and hurried in the direction that Ebed-melech had taken. After a few questions and some searching, I found him.

"Yahweh our God has just spoken to me," I told him. "He sent you a message – a reward for your bravery and godliness. He said:

" 'Go, and say to Ebed-melech the Ethiopian,
"Thus says the Lord of hosts,
the God of Israel:
Behold, I will fulfil my words
against this city
for harm and not for good,
and they shall be accomplished
before you on that day.
But I will deliver you on that day,
declares the Lord,
and you shall not be given
into the hand of the men

of whom you are afraid.
For I will surely save you,
and you shall not fall by the sword,
but you shall have your life as a prize of war,
because you have put your trust in me,
declares the Lord." ' "[39]

The look of relief on his face showed just how confident Ebed-melech was in the word of God.

If only my nation had such confidence in God.

ॐ

Weeks passed and the last items of food in the city were frantically consumed. The reports I heard suggested that hunger had made people consider anything that moved to be food. God's laws that defined animals as clean or unclean were being completely ignored by everyone. Apparently all of the livestock and larger animals in the city had disappeared long before. Dogs, mice and rats, lizards and frogs were all available at high prices in the markets, but very little else was.

Hunger led many to desperation – and I felt that I could understand why. After weeks of doing without food, I knew the torment of hunger. I knew what it was like to have thoughts of food filling every waking moment. I knew what it was like to dream of greedily eating a feast, only to wake up still desperate with hunger.

From the king to the poorest beggar, all were being consumed with hunger. Pregnant women lost their babies due to lack of food; newborn babies died because their mothers could give them no milk; the aged died from hunger and neglect.

---

[39] Jeremiah 39:16-18

Death was the close companion of everyone in the city, and horrific stories were passed from mouth to mouth.

I was hugely thankful when my mother came to visit me again. Once more, she had been quite sick. From the news that I had heard of conditions in the city over the last two months, I had never expected to see her again.

She walked into my room slowly, escorted by my brother Gemariah. Each step was taken with difficulty, but the same indomitable spirit still showed in her eyes.

"Mother!" I cried, and surprised myself by bursting into tears.

We embraced, and both of us wept, while rejoicing in the joy of meeting again.

"Oh, Jeremiah, my son! It is so good to see that you are still alive."

"I am amazed that *you* are alive. Have there been any deaths in the family or relatives or anyone else we know?"

"Mother is the only one we know over 70 who is still alive," said Gemariah bluntly. "And she is only just alive." There was a hint of anger and blame in his voice, clearly directed at me.

"Our neighbours have lost two young children," said my mother. "It was horrible to watch them fade away."

"And another neighbour a few houses away had already lost her husband in the fighting. Then just a few days ago, her child died – and there were questions about that," said Gemariah.

"What do you mean?"

"It's just what God predicted through Moses," said my mother.

"No!" I said in horror.

"Nobody is completely sure," said Gemariah, "but it seems most likely that she killed the baby and then ate it. There was no doubt about the fact that there was no body left to bury."

"How long will it be before Jerusalem is captured?" asked my mother.

"I don't know, but it can't be long. When did you last have anything to eat, mother?"

"Almost three weeks ago."

"For me it is just over four weeks ago, so I'm glad it's not that long for you."

"Well, you are the one who predicted all of this, Jeremiah," said Gemariah. "It's about time you started to accept some of the responsibility for all of these terrible things. Women eating their babies? It's inhuman – and without you, none of it would have happened."

"Jeremiah is just passing on God's messages, Gemariah," said my mother firmly. "Your argument is with God, not with Jeremiah."

"Don't be ridiculous, mother. I don't argue with God. You know that Yahweh is a God of love. And he said that he would put his name in Jerusalem forever. Forever hasn't finished yet."

"My son," said my mother, and her voice sounded even stronger, "God said that he would put his name in Jerusalem *if* Solomon and his descendants followed God's commands. They haven't. That's why the Chaldean army is camped outside the walls waiting for us to give up. And we will have to do so soon. We can't possibly last even one more week. But you can't blame Jeremiah for that – and don't criticise Yahweh either!"

Chapter 6

The end

July, 587 BC – the 11th year of King Zedekiah

There was nothing left for anyone to eat.

Even the king and his family – the life of the kingdom – had no food.

Outside the city, the Chaldeans waited, and the smells from their cooking fires tormented us. Was it deliberate that they often built fires upwind, just out of reach of the stones and arrows of the defenders, then cooked all manner of desirable food on them, the tantalising aromas of which wafted over the walls on the breezes, mocking the cravings of the starving inhabitants?

Night and day, our hunger would not leave us alone. Like pain, it was impossible ever to completely forget it.

The Chaldeans could have chosen to just sit there patiently waiting for us to give up, or die of starvation. My mother had been right that we couldn't have lasted another week. But as it was, the defence of the city lasted only three more days.

I was in prison when the city was ringed by Chaldean soldiers for the last time, but I was expecting it because I believed God's word. Early in the siege, however, many who did not believe God's word had hoped for relief: Egypt will come to save us, they cried. But Egypt hadn't come.

Eighteen months later, no-one had any hope of relief.

Terror was our constant companion.

Starvation was relentless, but predictable. Disease and pestilence were not, and the reports from the city were that many were dying every day. This, too, was just as God had predicted. He had said that he himself would fight against the city, striking man and beast with pestilence. There were no more animals left alive in the city: all had been killed, either by pestilence or by hungry citizens. Many of those who ate the dead bodies of the animals that died of these plagues – particularly the rats and mice – had died soon afterwards. God was spreading terror in the city.

Stones from catapults and arrows from archers were not predictable either. They delivered sudden death from above – and terror with it.

Chaldean battering rams can breach the strongest defences in the world, but the walls of Jerusalem had already endured countless attempts to shatter them. In places, Chaldean workmen had even piled earth against the walls to enable their soldiers to crest the wall and pour over into the city. Yet every attempt had been repulsed – so far. Nevertheless, within the palace complex and on either side of it – where the Chaldean attacks were most fierce – the houses near the wall had been desperately torn down, so that their rubble could be used in the defence of the city.

Walls were strengthened, buttressed, extended upwards – and for some time the improved defences held. But the terror did not go away.

The Chaldean army did not give up. The battering rams were moved to other sections of the wall. Probing, nudging, testing the strength of the wall, the alertness of the defence. The fearful defenders responded frenziedly to every offensive. Desperate. Despairing.

It seems that, however great one's terror may be, it can always grow stronger.

The Chaldean attacks were persistent – and then they found a weakness in the outer wall.

When I first started this diary, I knew that, if I was able to continue writing, I would eventually have to tell of the fall of Jerusalem. When I began to write, I never intended to let anyone read it; but after spending so much time on it, and trying throughout to explain exactly why such a disaster occurred, I have begun to wonder if I should present parts of it to people.

So many people have died, and yet the survivors still seem to wonder why! How could they possibly remain ignorant when God has spelled out the details so clearly?

Maybe this diary can help them to understand.

But to be able to explain the conclusion, I need to describe the destruction of Judah and how the events fulfilled God's warnings.

I could skip over it. It hurts to think about it, let alone write of it. But it was the fulfilment of what God had been threatening from the very beginning of my work for him. I began to write this diary because Johanan the son of Kareah refused to believe that God was speaking through me. He was not in the city when it fell. Maybe a description of the events can help to convince him that God works to fulfil his plans, not to match our desires.

For me, that final day – the ninth day of the fourth month of Zedekiah's eleventh year – began as many others had before it: a stone from a Chaldean catapult struck the pavement of the court of the guard, sending deadly splinters of stone flying through the air. This was not unusual.

Through a fog of sleep and the disorienting weakness of starvation, I heard screams of pain, followed by many shouts. I struggled slowly to my feet, then staggered to the door of my room. As I reached the door, another heavy shudder announced the arrival of a second stone some distance away. It was the start of the heaviest bombardment of the entire siege, continuing all day until it was no longer needed. Stones rained down on us from the various catapults surrounding the city and the earth shook almost constantly as each stone landed.

I opened my door and saw torches bobbing around in the courtyard as soldiers ran to and fro and the shouting continued. I went out, partly to see if I could do anything to help, and partly because I knew that I wouldn't be able to sleep any longer anyway, and didn't want to lie in bed feeling sorry for myself.

But by the time I was out in the courtyard, there was nothing I could do. One man had died when the first stone had bounced and struck him. Another had lost an eye as he watched uselessly for the danger he was unable to see coming in the darkness.

I would have sat with the injured man if he had let me, but he did not want a traitor looking after him.

There was not much to do as I waited. Many guards remained in the court, since it was the headquarters of the king's guards, and the king must always be protected.

The heavy bombardment continued and the sounds of battle rose.

Suddenly an officer ran into the courtyard, shouting, "We need everyone who can possibly be spared!"

"We're all meant to be staying to guard the palace," replied the officer of the guard.

"If you don't come to the wall now, there won't be any hope of defending the king here," snapped the officer. A sound of renewed fighting came from the direction of the Benjamin Gate, beyond the temple. The officer looked away, then turned back. "I must go," he said.

"Maybe we could spare a few men," said Omri, the officer of the guard, doubtfully. "But why do you need them?"

"They've been attacking the wall again, and have broken through the outer wall – Manasseh's wall.[40] Many men have been lost, but the rest of us fought off the Chaldeans and withdrew safely behind the inner wall. But now they're dragging the battering ram up to the inner wall. I don't think that wall will last very long if we let them get to work on it. We've got to stop them somehow. I'm going now. Come as soon as you can."

"Alright. I'll come with all the men we can possibly spare and leave my second in command in charge here."

The officer ran off while Omri quickly gathered those who could be spared and hurried after him.

The gate was closed behind them and the shouting continued to grow louder, accompanied by frequent screams of pain. The earth seemed to shake continually

---

[40] 2 Chronicles 33:14

as the titanic struggle continued. Soon, the repetitive sound of a battering ram was heard. The attempt to keep it away had obviously failed.

Time seemed almost to stand still as the volume of the shouting continued to rise, the bombardment continued and the rhythmic thud of the battering ram strengthened.

The soldiers remaining in the court of the guard were obviously fretting, eager to leave their passive posts to join the action they could hear so close by. But they must stay to protect the king.

An hour passed slowly as the noise grew slowly louder. Then a sudden rumble heralded some change. The battering ram fell silent and the sound of falling masonry drowned out the shouts of mingled triumph and terror. I found out later that this was the moment at which the battering ram broke through the inner wall, dislodging enough of the stones to allow the remainder of the wall to collapse on top of the ram and any men nearby. The defenders on top of the wall fell with it, and soon hordes of Chaldean soldiers were swarming in through the gap.

In the court of the guard, we heard the sounds of war spreading now across the city. Coming closer. The king's palace was likely to be one of the primary targets, and the soldiers left in the complex prepared to fight to the death, guarding their king. The city might be lost, but a recovery was always possible as long as the king remained alive and free.

I was left alone in the open courtyard – the only prisoner who was free to roam. I sat and waited. God's prohibition on prayer for my people still bound me, and all I could do was pray for those whom I loved, in the hope that God would accept that it was not a prayer for my people.

Soon I heard shouts coming from the palace gate, followed by the clash of swords. The twang of bowstrings showed that battle had been well and truly joined.

The open area in front of the palace was out of bounds for me, and the gate that led into the royal living quarters would probably have been closed to provide maximum defensive strength. The courtyard where I sat was expendable in the defence of the king – and so was I.

It was an eerie feeling: sitting alone, an expendable man in an expendable courtyard, while the sounds of warfare spread all around me. What was happening to my family, I wondered – my mother in particular. She was so old and helpless. Yet I too was helpless. Baruch: would he be in the temple? God had promised him safety through the upheaval that was now well underway. Ebedmelech also could be sure of his life, despite the disaster.

Yet I had no such guarantee, and it seemed unfair. I now believe that it was simply a lack of faith on my part: I should have been just as confident of my own safety as those two faithful helpers were of theirs. God does not abandon his own, even when they are weak, which at that moment I certainly was.

As I sat, a persistent noise began to come from the direction of the temple, and after a while I noticed that the gate that led from the court of the guard into the temple court was shaking and slowly seeming to bulge inwards. Although small, it was still a solid, heavy gate, and it took some time before the hinges finally tore out of the wall and the bulging gate fell across the pathway. Through the gap, I could see a group of about thirty Chaldean soldiers, shouting and waving their arms briefly in victory before running towards me, led by their commander, a young man with sword and shield.

I suppose that it was clear that an old, unarmed man sitting alone in an empty courtyard was no real threat, but I did not expect the respect with which I was treated.

"Old man," cried their leader in awkward Hebrew, stopping in front of me while his men spread out around the courtyard, searching for any possible dangers, "why are you sitting alone? Where are those who should guard your king?"

"They have gone to parts of the palace better suited for defence," I answered in Aramaic, and he looked relieved to hear me use his language. "I am a prisoner," I finished.

"A prisoner in the palace? You must have upset your king badly. What is your crime?"

"I am a prophet of Yahweh. I told the king that the Chaldean army would take the city."

The man looked interested. "What is your name?" he asked.

"Jeremiah," I answered.

"Ah, Jeremiah!" he said, pronouncing my name in the way that I had become used to from speakers of Aramaic. "We have heard about you. You have made our job of taking the city a little easier by suggesting that people should surrender instead of continuing to fight. The generals were so pleased with it that they treated the deserters much more kindly than we normally would."

"It was God's will. He wanted his people punished, not slaughtered."

"But most have fought. They will be slaughtered. To be honest, they are already being slaughtered."

A soldier approached. "Excuse me sir," he said. "We have found a locked gate that seems to lead into the rest of the palace, but it is very strong. There are defenders on the other side, sir. What shall we do?"

"Jeremiah, come with us. This area will soon become a battleground, and I am sure that the generals will not want you to be hurt. Come."

He rapped out some quick orders to his men to begin the attack on the gate, then led me into the temple courts. For the first time in more than eighteen months, I was not a prisoner of my own people. Instead, I was a prisoner of the Chaldeans, that bitter and hasty people. How would they treat me?

In the temple it was immediately clear that hard fighting had taken place, but that the battle was almost over. The pavement that I had seen flowing with the blood of festival sacrifices now flowed with the blood of priests and prophets, soldiers and officials, parents and children. A sanctuary no longer, God's temple was now filled with death. As the priests had filled God's house with lifeless idols, so God had now filled the house with their own dead bodies. Their white linen clothes had been worn in proud rebellion against God. Now, torn and bloodied, the linen clothed only scattered, silent corpses.

I had known for 40 years that this devastation was coming, but that knowledge had in no way prepared me for the reality I saw spread out before me that day. Many of the bodies, unrecognisable though they now were, were probably men I knew. Indeed, some must be my close relatives, but the faces I could see were all distorted into anonymity by terrifying, violent death.

Shouting came suddenly from a passageway and I saw two Chaldean soldiers being attacked by four soldiers of Judah who must have been hiding in ambush in a storage room. A Chaldean soldier responded with disciplined speed, and one Judean soldier screamed as he fell to the ground. Another of King Zedekiah's men ran forward and seemed to slip. Perhaps he slipped on blood, or maybe it was the weakness of starvation; whatever the cause, his swinging blade struck another of his fellows in the neck and the blood spurted, horribly. As they both fell together, the other Chaldean soldier calmly thrust them both through with two clinical strokes. The remaining Judean soldier did not seek to run, but now he was outnumbered two to one, and he didn't seem to see the thrusting sword of one of the Chaldean soldiers as he stepped forward. Soon all four Judean soldiers lay dead on the pavement, and it was hard to explain why except by remembering the words of God:

"Thus says the Lord, the God of Israel:
Behold, I will turn back the weapons of war
that are in your hands
and with which you are fighting
against the king of Babylon
and against the Chaldeans
who are besieging you outside the walls.
And I will bring them together
into the midst of this city.
I myself will fight against you
with outstretched hand and strong arm,
in anger and in fury and in great wrath."[41]

What hope had Judah in the battle when God was fighting against them?

These things I saw in only a very short time as the Chaldean captain led me through the temple courts. We crossed the pavement towards the Benjamin Gate of the temple, threading our way through the fallen bodies as if they were so many thorn bushes on the hills outside Anathoth.

As we walked around one body that lay in a pool of blood, I saw that the man was moving slightly. He was still alive. I stopped and bent to touch him. I am no doctor, but felt that I must try to do something to help.

---

[41] Jeremiah 21:4-5

But the Chaldean captain took my hand and pulled me upright. "Don't waste your time," he said curtly. "He won't last long, and I'm in a hurry. I need to take you to my superior officer."

We left the dying man behind, among all the bodies and blood. Judah was paying for her sins. Oh, how she was paying!

As we passed beyond the temple, I could see the breach in the city wall. It was peculiar to able to see into the Valley of the Kidron over the ruins of a wall that had blocked that view all my life. Chaldean soldiers were everywhere – and so were the bodies. Men, women and even children had met death in every possible position, and now lay in mute testimony to the many prophecies I had delivered since that momentous day when God had first spoken to me on my seventeenth birthday. The work of a prophet had not turned out to be at all what I had expected. I had not expected a glamorous life, but I had never expected this. How many of the dead bodies that now littered the streets had heard God's warnings from me and ignored them?

It all seemed so pointless. So wasteful.

God had never wanted them to die. He had given warning after warning, not only by me, but also by many other prophets. Opportunities to repent. Descriptions of what repentance meant and how their lives must change.

All that work had gone to waste. Nothing could be changed now. The disaster was working its way through Jerusalem. The shouting that still filled the city showed that the fighting was not over. As I watched, more and more Chaldean troops marched in through the breach in the wall and spread out all through the city. Other men were working on clearing away the rubble that had been used to strengthen the Benjamin Gate. Within an hour or two it would be cleared, and troops could flood into the city more quickly. Presumably the other gates around the city would be cleared also, as soon as the defenders were overrun. It would not be long.

Many, many more bundles of clothes would fill the streets and houses of Jerusalem before night came.

As I stood gazing about me, the Chaldean captain who was leading me searched for his superior officer, but without success. Apparently the man had led a strong force of Chaldean soldiers down past the palace, putting down resistance as he went.

"Come with me," said the captain. "I'm afraid that you'll be killed if I leave you here. It's a dangerous place to be at the moment, with new troops coming in all the time, looking for battle. By the way, my name is Belibni."

We retraced our steps and passed through the temple, this time leaving it by the gate through which I had fled many years before when escaping a woman from that accursed room of pictures.[42] It was so long ago, but so closely connected with this day's events. If only the nation had turned around when the great king Josiah showed them the way to God. If only Josiah, our bright hope, had lived to lead his nation a little longer. What difference would another ten years have made?

Sadly, though, the truth is that it would probably not have made any difference at all.

Even when Josiah was there, the nation's heart had never really turned fully to God.

And now this was the result.

We headed down into the city, passing the palace where massed Chaldean troops were attacking the gates, meeting stiff resistance from King Zedekiah's best forces.

---

[42] See Volume 2 – As Good As It Gets, Chapter 4.

By that time my mind was numbed by the sheer magnitude of the massacre I was witnessing. I could not even begin to estimate the numbers of inhabitants who had woken this morning, but would wake no more. At least their hunger would no longer trouble them.

As we hurried towards the southern end of the city, we began to see even more dead bodies. Some were those of Chaldean soldiers, but most were those of the people of the city. These were not men who had fallen in battle – they were people killed in cold blood by men on a violent rampage. Young and old filled the roadways and lay slumped in every doorway. At times it was hard to find a way through the street without treading on bodies. The city was the strongest in the kingdom, so, of course, it had been full to overflowing when the siege had begun. Now their attempts to escape to the safety of Jerusalem had proved futile – death had found them anyway.

As Belibni and I approached the Potsherd Gate, we were at last catching up with the tail end of the Chaldean strike force. From our position we could see over the heads of the crowded mass of soldiers wielding swords and spears against unarmed men, women and children. Beyond them we saw how desperation can speed up a task. This gatehouse, like all the others, had been filled with rubble to resist the Chaldean battering rams, yet it had already been cleared by the bare hands of the fleeing inhabitants. As I watched, I saw them push the gates open.

There, beyond the gates, I saw their final doom awaiting them.

Outside, in the Valley of the Son of Hinnom, cursed Topheth, called by God "The Valley of Slaughter", the massed army of the Chaldeans stood and waited silently – implacable, deadly.

Pushed forward by those behind, the crowd surged out of the gate.

Bright swords and spears glinted in the late afternoon sun, but soon their brightness was bathed in blood.

For the people of Jerusalem, there was death in front and death behind – terror on every side.

The Valley of Slaughter earned its name that afternoon.

Eventually, darkness fell on Jerusalem, yet blood continued to flow in the streets.

Chapter 7

Life and death

Later that night, I was sent back to the court of the guard. Belibni, the Chaldean captain who had been taking care of me, had eventually found his commander near the Potsherd Gate and they had agreed that I should be kept safe. They had also decided that the best place for that might actually be the court of the guard – once the resistance in the palace had been overcome.

I am sure that I will never forget that day. How could I forget the horrific slaughter of my people? Men and women, caught between two armies; defenceless and terrified; uncomprehending and helpless.

Abraham's descendants have always been confident of God's protection. The entire nation counted on it at a subconscious level. Although very few ever made any effort to serve God as he required or as their father Abraham had, the entire nation was still sure that destruction on such a scale could never, ever, come upon them.

Centuries of history had cemented this certainty into the national consciousness, and although the destruction of Samaria had briefly unsettled it, self-righteous Judah had a perfect explanation for that disaster!

Yet now, even children had been trampled in the stampede of terror, countless bodies lying broken in the streets once the crush had passed.

I cannot describe the horror of seeing death on such a vast and impersonal scale, yet reflected in the eyes of individuals who were close enough for me to see their suffering. Following Belibni, I was close to the horrific action when he found his superior officer and discussed my future. As I watched, some of the victims found the energy to scream, but most faced their death with silent resignation, despite the terrified disbelief on their faces. No-one seemed to find either strength or opportunity for resistance. Completely unarmed, with their doom so unexpected, the people of Jerusalem were herded to their deaths and killed without mercy.

The Chaldean soldiers were angry assailants. Eighteen months of their lives had been spent camped outside a rebellious city, and now that their opportunity for revenge had come, they were in a frenzy of brutality.

The scene unfolded as I waited. Despite the press, I occasionally saw men that I recognised – including some who had held market stalls in areas where I had frequently delivered God's messages. These stall-holders had generally tolerated me, and some had even talked to me from time to time about my messages, but really, they were just the same as everyone else in the city – utterly deaf to the words and warnings of Yahweh. That day, I saw them cut down. I witnessed their punishment.

One of these men was in the gatehouse of the Potsherd Gate as the soldiers in the city were driving the crowd out through the gate, striking down those who were nearest if they did not move quickly enough. This man – whose name I never knew – was quite tall, and in that instant, he glanced towards me over the heads of the crowd. Our eyes met and recognition was mutual. Seeing me standing behind the Chaldean soldiers and next to an officer caused fierce anger to spread across his face. He screamed one word, which carried faintly even over the noise of the slaughter, and there was no doubt that it was directed at me: "Traitor!"

Almost as he spoke, he was struck down, and I saw his body fall with the others.

At times, I have felt great anger against my people – both anger with individuals and anger at the institutions of the nation. Yet when I saw their doom, all I could feel for them was pity, and the beginnings of anger against God. But above all, I felt pity for myself.

Through my work, I had endured, and some would say earned, the hatred of my stubborn nation. Yet what had I achieved? What was the point of suffering so much when no-one had listened anyway?

It was a feeling of self-pity and criticism of Yahweh that was to grow in the days and weeks that followed. I'm ashamed of it now, and glad that God is constant and forgiving. I'm not trying to excuse it, either, but at that time I was overwhelmed; my emotions strained beyond breaking point. God had promised me strength, but I chose not to seek it.

Eventually, long after darkness had fallen, Belibni led me back towards the palace and the court of the guard. As we walked along dark streets accompanied by a few soldiers with torches, I saw that many of the bodies had been dragged together and stacked in piles, no longer recognisable in the darkness as people. Fires were burning in isolated locations across the city, but there had not been the wholesale burning that I had expected in fulfilment of God's words. That was yet to come.

I was utterly exhausted, and found it very hard to climb the streets towards the palace. Hunger still gnawed at me and I felt as though I was walking in a nightmare.

Once again, I was surprised by Belibni's concern for me, as he slowed his pace to a speed that I could cope with, and even offered me a mouthful of dried fruit from his pouch. Slowly we approached the gates of the palace, around which large numbers of Chaldean soldiers sat or stood, looking quite relaxed. There were no sounds of fighting, no signs of an ongoing struggle. The gatehouse lay in ruins, as I had seen it in my dream, and the courtyard gates lay broken on the ground.

Seeing an officer he knew, Belibni asked, "Excuse me, sir, has the palace been taken?"

"Yes, but not in quite the way we wanted, Belibni. The ostrich has run."

"But how?"

"Apparently he escaped through a gate and a tunnel – and lots of his men with him. A clever setup, really. Within the palace walls there is a garden, and from there a hidden gate leads into the space between the inner and outer walls. From the look of it, it was designed as an escape route for just such a time as this. Then, further along in the gap between the walls, there was another hidden entrance, this time to a tunnel."

"But how could they do it without being seen?"

The senior officer didn't seem to be in any hurry to tell his story, nor did he appear to have noticed me in the dark. "It seems that the defenders waited until they were sure that the city had been taken before they began to put their plan into effect," he said. "I suppose it was pretty obvious that the city was lost when all of our top brass were gathered in the middle of the gate in full view of the upper levels of the palace. It was just before it got dark: Nergal-sar-ezer, Samgar-nebu, the Rab-saris, the Rab-mag, and all the rest of them.[43]

"Anyway, their soldiers continued to defend the palace doggedly until after dark, making sure that any move on our part was met with an immediate response. Then, once it was dark, they must have smuggled the king out of the gate, with most of the defenders at his heels.[44] The few defenders left behind continued to respond to our forays. Would you believe it? – they tricked us for almost two hours! It wasn't until we decided to begin a major offensive that the weakness of their defence was shown. Even so, they cleverly left some snipers hidden around, ready to deliver unexpected slingstones from the upper floors. It certainly wasn't all easy, but soon we could tell that most of the defenders had gone. After that we pressed them hard and took the palace quickly."

"But how did you find out *where* they had gone?" asked Belibni.

"It was really just a bit of good luck, I suppose – or our gods helping us, as the soothsayers would suggest. Naturally we scoured the palace inside and out trying to find out where they had gone. All of the women in the palace were amazingly calm, and they did their best to mislead us. Nevertheless, we were confident that the escape route was most likely to be outside the palace buildings, and so it proved to be.

"We quickly found the garden and searched it carefully, but the defenders had hidden the gate by covering it over with branches. We wouldn't have had a hope of finding it if one of our men hadn't had a very

---

[43] Jeremiah 39:3

[44] Jeremiah 39:4

sharp eye. He saw a footprint – just one – in the middle of the branches that hid the gate. He quickly pulled at the branches and, lo and behold, they came away completely, and there was the door hidden behind. That was all well and good, but we still wouldn't have found the entrance to the tunnel except that one of our men who was searching the area between the two walls tripped over a rock and fell. Doesn't sound like a good thing, you might say, but it was right next to a place where a tower was built directly on top of the rock. It was completely dark, so he was holding a torch, and as he was getting up, he saw in the dim light, a small piece of material caught in a gap between two rocks. Once again, it was an amazing piece of luck. He pulled at the rock and it came out in his hand. A little more searching and he had found the hidden passageway. We don't know where it leads yet, but we have men searching it.

"Oh, and by the way, Belibni, make sure that no-one hears about this until their king is captured or killed."

Immediately, Belibni turned and looked at me, standing in the dark behind him. "Jeremiah," he said, "did you hear all that?"

"Yes," I said.

"Who is this?" asked the senior officer, suspiciously.

"You know the Judean prophet we heard about who was telling the people to surrender? Well, this is the man: Jeremiah."

"Can we trust him? Or should we kill him?"

"Can we trust you, Jeremiah?"

"Yes, you can trust me," I said with a sigh. "And I can tell you that you will catch our king, too. The great God Yahweh has told me that Zedekiah will not escape, so it is sure to happen that way. It wasn't luck that you found that footprint, nor was it luck that your soldier fell over and found the passage.   King Zedekiah cannot escape Yahweh."

"I have heard that your god can predict the future. Is it really true?"

"Yes, it is. Just wait and see," I said.

"Back in Babylon King Nebuchadnezzar has some Judean prophets. Sometimes they please him, but other times they infuriate him. You know, they say that once he threw three of them into his furnace, but they just wouldn't burn! He had to ask them politely to come out. Those three and a friend of theirs are basically running the whole province of Babylon now – and doing a good job, too, from what I hear. Still, it seems strange to defeat a nation and then use some of its people to run your own provinces!"

"Is one of those men called Daniel?"

"I think the king calls him a much more normal name, 'Belteshazzar' maybe, but I know that most people call him a different name – and 'Daniel' does ring a bell, so I guess that must be it. If only you Judeans would use nice simple names like ours, things would be much easier, eh, Belibni?"

"Yes, sir. And yes, I believe the man's Hebrew name is Daniel."

I was pleased to hear that Daniel was still in an important position in Babylon, but his influence must be worth nothing here in Jerusalem, as his people were being treated like so many rats to be exterminated.

"Now, Belibni," the officer continued, "what are you doing with this prophet of yours?"

"My boss suggested that I should see if he could be kept safe in the court of the guard".

"Well, I can tell you that it's free of enemy combatants. But it would still be best to wait an hour or so before you leave him there. We're still busy getting rid of the dead bodies from there and the courtyard here. Not many of ours, I'm glad to say, but lots of theirs. Tonight we're just keeping the palace locked down, but tomorrow the top brass will formally take it over and decide what to do with the ex-king's family. A bit of a victory celebration, really, and the bigwigs don't like to have dead bodies lying around when they are eating their morning snacks." He laughed mirthlessly.

"Where are they taking the bodies, sir?"

"Well, of course, our dead will get a proper burial with all the rites that a Chaldean soldier deserves, but we've arranged for carts to come and collect all of the Judean bodies and dump them outside the gate they call the Potsherd Gate. We won't have enough room to bury them all in the city, so they'll just end up buried along with the others that were killed today in the valley of slaughter outside the gate."

It sent shivers up and down my spine to hear these men casually discussing the actions and decisions that would fulfil God's prophecies in such fine detail. The Valley of Ben Hinnom had already become a place of slaughter, just as God had predicted,[45] and now it would also be used as a burial place because there was no room left for burials in the city. This, too, God had predicted.[46]

The discussion ended soon afterwards, and Belibni was clearly at a loose end as we walked away from the palace. Suddenly, an idea seemed to occur to him and he asked me, "Do you have any close family in the city, Jeremiah? Parents? Siblings?"

I was touched by his kindness and replied, "Until just a few days ago, my mother and brother were living only a

---

[45] Jeremiah 19:6
[46] Jeremiah 7:32

short distance from here, quite close to the temple. Could we go and see if we can find out what has happened to them?"

"Certainly, as long as the area where they live is safe," he responded, calling a few of his soldiers to accompany us, holding their torches aloft. I led them past the southern end of the temple to where Gemariah's house was. As we approached, it was clear, even in the darkness, that the house had been badly damaged by fire. Opening the front door, I could see a body lying silently and peacefully in the shadows just inside. One of the soldiers came forward to help me and, by the light of his torch, I realised that the darkness had given a false impression of peace. While still recognisable, the body was quite badly damaged, although I could not tell whether the damage had occurred before or after death. It was my brother, Gemariah, and I wept at this final loss of the brother who had been my friend as a child. Our choices had long ago led us along separate paths, and towards the end I feel sure that he hated me, and may well have been involved in some of the later plans to kill me. But I was still heartbroken to find him dead, and took a long time to control myself. After that, I went further into the house, my path lit by the Chaldean soldier's torch. Much of the house had been burned and the roof had fallen in, so it was not possible to search properly in the dark, but there was no sign of anyone else, dead or alive. The heat of the fire lingered and in some places, smoke still curled slowly upward.

I went out again and Belibni asked me what I had found.

"I found my brother – dead," I answered. "There may also be others under the collapsed roof. Maybe I can search better in the light tomorrow. I guess that my mother must be dead too."

"Couldn't we ask in the houses around to see if anyone knows what has happened to your mother?" asked Belibni. "Someone will probably know."

All through the afternoon, Belibni had been with me, attending me, protecting me, giving me information I could never have found by myself, and now, finally, belatedly, it began to occur to me that maybe this was God's way of caring for me. It made me feel ashamed of myself. Throughout the disaster, as others died in their tens of thousands, I had not only been protected, but also shown the accuracy of God's prophecies. Yet I had spent much of that time feeling sorry for myself and wondering if I would be safe.

I took Belibni's advice and went to the house next door. For several minutes I tried every way I could think of to get a response from within, but the door was locked and nothing but silence greeted my calls.

Finally, one of the soldiers took a hand by issuing a brutal warning. "We are about to burning down your house!" he shouted. "Bringing of the torches." It was poor and heavily accented Hebrew, but it did the trick.

"Wait!" cried a terrified voice from within. "Don't do that."

"Then let me in," I said. "I am Jeremiah, the son of Hilkiah, and I'm looking for my mother."

"Are you really Jeremiah?"

"I am."

"Why are you with Chaldean soldiers?"

"They are helping me to find my mother."

"What will they do to us?"

"Don't worry, you'll be alright," I said, confident at last of God's protection in the midst of devastation.

"Your mother is here, but she's very weak."

"Open the door and let me see her."

A few more questions went back and forth and then the door slowly opened and a man emerged cautiously from the darkened interior of the house.

"We haven't dared to light any lamps. We have been hiding in silence ever since we rescued your mother after the soldiers left."

I went into the house, lighting a lamp from one of the torches. The soldiers were on high alert – unwilling to enter the house unless with their swords unsheathed. Belibni thought it would be best for everyone if they stayed outside, so I went in by myself to see my mother. She was lying on a bed and didn't move as I bent over her and gently kissed her cheek.

Her eyes opened.

"They killed him, Jeremiah," she said in a shaky voice.

"I know, Mother," I answered, and found that my voice was shaky too.

"He wouldn't listen to you. And now he's dead."

"Yes. Most people won't listen to prophets unless they are saying things that everyone wants to hear. And when the prophet is your brother, it seems to be harder still. Neither of my brothers would listen to me, and now it's too late. I can't do anything else."

"What will happen to us now, son?"

"I don't know. But God has been looking after us, hasn't he? You were rescued and so was I."

"Jeremiah," called Belibni's voice from outside.

I went out again quickly. "Yes?" I asked.

"Is your mother well enough to be carried to the court of the guard?"

"Yes, I think she'll be well enough. It's amazing really. She is 86 years old and hasn't had any food to eat for at least two weeks, yet she is still alive and alert."

"No food? Why?"

"Didn't you know that there is no food left in the city? Lots of people have already died of starvation and disease, yet my mother has survived."

"So that is why all of the defenders are so weak?"

"I suppose so."

"We need to get some food for you both, then."

I was amazed at the strength of my reaction to his suggestion. Even on a day when such carnage was all around me, thoughts of food had filled every pathway and corner of my mind except when the slaughter was right in front of me. For weeks, my every waking moment had been prey to irresistible dreams of delectable foodstuffs, and now, as Belibni made his generous suggestion, I felt that I could taste the food already. I hate to admit it, but if food had been set in front of me at that moment, I doubt that I could have forced myself to share it with anybody.

These dreams of food continued to haunt me as the Chaldean soldiers ordered the people in the house to carry my mother gently on a bed to the court of the guard.

What love Yahweh shows to his weak, blind servants!

Throughout the day, Yahweh had cared for me in every detail, yet I had not recognised it until the very end. Finally, however, I could see that I was alive only through his care. After all the danger and death that had surrounded me, I acknowledged that my mother too was not only alive, but with me in a safe place – and all because of Yahweh's meticulous solicitude.

Chapter 8

Nebuchadnezzar's orders

"Have some food!"

For a moment, as I struggled to wake up, I thought it was just another dream and that there would be no food in sight once I had rubbed the sleep from my eyes.

But no, Belibni was standing in the doorway with a servant carrying some bread and wine.

"There is enough for your mother as well," he continued. The joy of knowing that my mother was safe sprang up in me again, though I still felt the confusion of not quite knowing what was real and what had been mere dreams.

Glancing across the room, I saw the bed that had been set up for my mother when we had returned to my room in the court of the guard late the previous night, and the sight helped me to get my bearings.

By that time I was awake enough to think more clearly and remember the events of the day before. Gemariah, my brother, was dead. How many more people that I knew had died with the end of the siege?

I pushed the thought away and concentrated on the very real delight of food.

Our return to the court of the guard on the previous night had been too late for any food to be fetched for us from outside the city, so we had gone to bed still longing for food, but with the assurance that food would arrive with the new day.

Bread can seem a very plain food at times, but I had not seen bread for more than four weeks, and it looked like a royal feast. I crossed to my mother's bed and shook her gently.

"Mother," I called, "they have brought us some food." I marvelled at her toughness as slowly she woke up and rolled over, still alive despite conditions that had killed so many who were less than half her age.

"It is amazing that your mother is alive, Jeremiah," said Belibni. "Make sure that you take good care of her."

"I'll do my best as Yahweh provides the opportunities."

"And King Nebuchadnezzar, too. We have sent enquiries to find out what we should do with you, and we should get a reply soon. In the meantime, we will leave you to eat your food in your own way."

"Thank you."

"Just a word of warning, Jeremiah: we have seen great problems before in other places when people have started to eat again after they haven't eaten for a long time. Take it slowly and cautiously. Don't eat too much at once or it could kill you."

We eagerly took the bread and wine we were offered. As I looked at it, the food had an irresistible beauty such as only starvation could ever bestow on such plain fare! Its delectable, homely smell filled my nostrils, reminding me of a day in my childhood when I had been playing on the hillside near Anathoth, and all nature had seemed to be filled with beauty and pleasure. On my return home, I had arrived just in time to see my mother easing some newly-baked bread out of the oven, filling the house with a delectable smell that was almost strong enough to taste – even to touch. That day, I had shared some fresh bread with my mother and we had sat together companionably, a still-young mother with her youngest son, happy, with all the hopes and dreams of life still intact.

As promised, Belibni left us alone so that we could eat in private, and we sat together to eat once again, this time in a prison room, a very old widow with her one remaining son, survivors of a nation that had been broken down by the judgement of God.

The first mouthful of bread was pure savoury perfection as the gently rough texture of an exquisitely cooked loaf rested on my tongue, the flavour slowly filling my mouth.

I took Belibni's warning seriously and did my best to make sure that neither my mother nor I ate too much or too quickly. Yet still, the joy of a hunger satisfied filled our hearts, and the memory of the terrors we had witnessed receded for the moment.

For my mother and me, the court of the guard was an oasis in which we were kept safe. There were few people in the court of the guard at that point, but more were brought in from time to time. These newcomers told us stories of a city still dying of starvation. The Chaldeans had food, but none of the Judean survivors were being given any. None but Chaldeans were permitted to leave the city, and all others were being forced to help dispose of the thousands of dead bodies. Men carried or dragged the dead bodies of their neighbours to the nearest place where they could be buried. But all the available places were quickly being filled, and time was running out for disposing of the bodies. It was summer, and the summer sun in Jerusalem is fierce. Already the piles of bodies that lay on every street were corrupting. Carrion-eating birds were gathered around the bodies and the dead were not being left to rest in peace.

The reports in the last days of the siege had stated that animals were completely absent from the city, but the lure of a glut of food had proved irresistible – rats and mice were back with a vengeance. Dogs also roamed the streets and helped themselves to parts of any corpses that were not closely guarded – and that was most of them.

Idolatry and faithlessness had brought war, and now war had brought unimaginable death and destruction.

CR

More dreams and prophecies were fulfilled that day, and had things not been so dire, I could have laughed at the frustration I had felt over the years when so many prophecies had seemed so far from fulfilment. Now, after 40 years, they were all being fulfilled in such a rush that it was hard to keep up with them all. Every new person to whom I spoke seemed to mention new details that fulfilled yet more of the oracles God had laid upon me.

That morning, my dream about Zedekiah's wives and children being presented to the leaders of Babylon was fulfilled, just a short distance from my room. We heard the sounds of the celebration, including the strange-sounding music played by Chaldean musicians on instruments with which I was unfamiliar.

News of Zedekiah's capture came also, as I had expected,[47] but the king was not brought back to Jerusalem – King Nebuchadnezzar was already making arrangements to move on to other urgent projects. Instead, Zedekiah was to be taken to Riblah in the land of Hamath, there to meet Nebuchadnezzar, to whom he had promised so much, only to break his oath. Riblah was the place to which Pharaoh Neco had summoned King Jehoahaz, Zedekiah's brother, 22 years earlier, and where he had bound him in chains.[48] Now Nebuchadnezzar was to deal with Zedekiah there, and I knew that he would take him to Babylon as God had promised.[49] If only Zedekiah had listened to God's warnings and surrendered!

As I sat in the court of the guard and thought, I was very glad to have my mother there with me. She had always been my greatest supporter, my most careful listener. Now, she asked me about the prophecies that had been fulfilled on that devastating day when Jerusalem had fallen, and the others that were continuing to be fulfilled in its aftermath.

My memory of God's words was still as strong as ever. The words were still written indelibly on the wall of my mind, fiery letters of warning and condemnation that often glowed more brightly when their messages were particularly appropriate. Over time, though, the words of God had become more difficult to scan as the sheer number of words grew. I did my best to try to organise them in my mind, remembering key themes and words so that I knew where to scan the wall to find the words that I wanted – and as long as I stayed near to God in my thoughts, the task was not difficult.

---

[47] Jeremiah 38:18

[48] 2 Kings 23:33

[49] Jeremiah 32:4-5

At this time, however, it was becoming increasingly difficult to find the words, and I find it hard to explain why. God's words were being fulfilled, and that was good – but something was badly wrong.

Maybe I was beginning to believe some of the things I had heard so often. Maybe I felt that the fact that I had food while my countrymen did not confirmed that I was a traitor. Whatever it was, I was not happy, and did not feel that I was altogether on the right side.

It was fortunate that my mother was with me, or I might have made a complete fool of myself.

We talked about the prophecies, and I could still repeat to her the words from my very earliest message, 40 years before. Some of the words were glowing brightly, and ordinarily I would have watched with fascination as God showed me how his words were related to what was going on that day in Jerusalem. But my heart wasn't in it, and I didn't take the opportunity. Not only that, but I didn't concentrate on using his words in my conversations either, even though I had always found that to be the best way to stay by God's side as he fulfilled his plans for my people.

I can't explain why it would happen, but I was starting to feel closer to my people than to God. How ridiculous! Throughout 40 years I had often longed for them to be punished quickly and wondered at the delay. I had complained that God was letting them off lightly. Yet now I was slowly moving towards approving of their folly.

It wasn't helped by the sneering and hatred that was shown by all of the people whom the Chaldeans brought into the court of the guard. I had grown very used to the word "traitor", but familiarity didn't make it hurt any less. God had promised to make me as immovable as a pillar of iron, but my stubborn resolution was crumbling because I was letting their attitudes affect me. 40 years of faith was in danger of falling to pieces – in danger of being utterly wasted.

It was about a week later that Belibni brought me the news.

Nebuzaradan and other very senior officers would be coming to see me very soon, he said, and he looked at me almost in awe that such important men would come to see *me*.

I had only a very short time to make myself presentable before the call came. Belibni led me through the palace into the chamber of the former chief of the king's army. It was a large room, and three Chaldean officers, whose insignia and demeanour announced them to be important men, were sitting waiting for me.

"You are Jeremiah, the prophet of Yahweh?" asked the one who was obviously the most important.

"Yes, sir," I responded.

"King Nebuchadnezzar has ordered us to look after you well. I am Nebuzaradan, chief of the guard, and these" – turning towards his two companions – "are Nebushazban the Rab-saris[50] and Nergal-sar-ezer the Rab-mag.[51] The king has entrusted us with making sure that you are taken care of. From what I hear, some of our junior officers have already been doing that on their own initiative." He turned and smiled approvingly at Belibni as he spoke, and it was clear that the latter's chances of promotion had improved significantly.

"Thank you," I said. I couldn't think what I had done to warrant such special treatment, and somehow it didn't even occur to me that this was simply God's amazing care in action.

---

[50] Rab-saris may mean chief of the officers.
[51] Rab-mag probably means chief of the magi.

"I understand that you have been in prison for almost two years because of your work. What would you like to do now? Tell us and we will arrange it."

"I don't know, sir," I said slowly and confusedly. "I would have to think about it some more."

"Well, you can have time to think about it, but you could probably be a great help to us in the city. Maybe you could help to calm down the hotheads who will try to continue the war just as soon as they get some food in their bellies."

"You could also help Gedaliah," said the man who had been introduced as Nebushazban, the Rab-saris. "King Nebuchadnezzar has appointed him as governor over the land, but he will have a hard time directing the people by himself. There are so few of your leaders left at any organisational level."

"I am no leader of the people," I answered bitterly. "All of them hate me."

"I'm not really surprised," said Nergal-sar-ezer, the Rab-mag. "Nobody likes a traitor, and that's what I have heard them call you."

I closed my eyes for a moment and then stared down at the floor. I had no idea what to say – he was right.

"Do you know Gedaliah, the son of Ahikam?" asked Nebushazban.

"Yes, sir," I answered, looking up. "Our families have been friendly for generations."

"Then you should go and stay with him," said Nebuzaradan. "He should be able to keep you safe from the people."

"Did he and his family listen to your warnings?" asked Nebushazban.

"Not really."

"Not even when they started to come true?"

"No, sir. Not even my own family would listen."

"It's extraordinary," said the Rab-saris, looking across at his fellow-officers in puzzlement.

"I hear that you have been warning your nation that this disaster is coming for more than 40 years," said Nebuzaradan. "How did you know what was coming? The Rab-mag here would always like to know how to read the future more reliably. But then, maybe it doesn't matter if they wouldn't listen to you anyway."

"Yahweh our God told me exactly what to say."

"We have another prophet from Judah back in Babylon who says the same thing. And he has the ear of the king too."

"Yes," said Nergal-sar-ezer, "the king always listens to Daniel, and he really does seem to know things that only the gods could know." I wasn't sure whether it was envy or admiration in the voice of the Rab-mag.

Suddenly it occurred to me that young Daniel, whose faith had impressed me so much when he was a teenager, was now helping to protect *me* by his faith – even from such a great distance.

For the moment, the knowledge encouraged me, and I agreed to join Gedaliah as he set up his new administration.

After a little more discussion we parted ways, Nebuchadnezzar's officers to report to him that I had been cared for, and I to prepare to leave the court of the guard – ready to enjoy freedom and life in the midst of a city of defeat and death.

Chapter 9

Fire among the ruins

"And you,
O profane wicked one,
prince of Israel,
whose day has come,
the time of your final punishment,
thus says the Lord God:
Remove the turban and take off the crown.
Things shall not remain as they are.
Exalt that which is low,
and bring low that which is exalted.
A ruin, ruin, ruin I will make it."

Ezekiel 21:25-27

As it turned out, freedom gave me little pleasure. At that time, I could not leave the city, and most of the surviving Judeans were very antagonistic towards me. Limited food was available for my mother and me, but it must be eaten in areas that were guarded by Chaldean soldiers, or violent theft was a very real possibility. The very fact that I could get food when many others could not was another trigger for accusations of cowardice and treason.

It seemed as though I was being offered freedom but then being told that I must be willing to give up everything that made freedom *freedom* in order to remain safe!

My mother and I were supposedly free to go wherever we wanted within Jerusalem, but we had been strongly advised by the Chaldeans to stay close to Gedaliah, the son of Ahikam, as he began to set up a new administration in Jerusalem under their direction.

He had been given control over some buildings that had formerly been used in the administration of the city and had not been damaged too badly during the siege or its conclusion. Some sections of these buildings had been converted to living quarters, and it was to these that Gedaliah directed us when I went to him with my mother. Nebuzaradan had already instructed him to take care of us, and I was grateful for that.

Although the siege was over, the city itself was still critically short of food. What food was available fed the victors first, then their helpers. Many who had survived the siege and its aftermath were still dying of starvation and the diseases of the siege.

Over time, further supplies would enter the city from the surrounding camps, carried in by some of the newly enslaved inhabitants, but the Chaldeans seemed to be in no hurry.

Once we had established ourselves in our new lodgings, I left my mother in her room and returned to Gedaliah. I wanted to find out what the Chaldeans had planned for the city and how that would fit in with what God had announced through me. God's words had included the complete destruction of the city, but this clearly had not happened. Not yet, anyway.

Was God showing mercy to his people, I wondered? Were the prophecies which had earned me such hatred not to be fulfilled anyway?

"Is your mother satisfied with her room?" Gedaliah asked when I rejoined him.

"Yes, she is very pleased and is now having a rest."

"Your mother is an amazing survivor!"

"She is – and God has cared for her through some terrible times."

"So many deaths among the young and strong, yet one old lady continues to survive. What a contrast."

"God predicted the deaths and devastation," I said.

"I suppose so. But all of your opponents were so sure that your words were wrong – I must admit that I wasn't so sure about them myself."

"Are you sure now?"

"I'm sure that you were right, but I'm not sure that I understand what is happening. My parents and my teachers all taught me that God is the God of Israel. Everyone said that Jerusalem was his city and that he had put his name in his house forever. If that's the case, how could such a disaster happen?"

"Right back when Solomon built the temple, God warned us that he would stay there only as long as we obeyed his commands. But everyone wants to remember the promise and forget the conditions."

"But in the past, we had leaders like Moses and Samuel, prophets who prayed for the nation. Have you been praying for Judah, Jeremiah?"

"No. God told me that I was not allowed to."

"So even in all this disaster, you haven't been praying for God to relent?"

"No. Most of the time I have obeyed his command."

"Would Moses have obeyed such a command? Would Samuel?"

"Of course they would. But they lived in different times."

"Maybe they just cared more about their nation!"

I hadn't expected such an attack from Ahikam's son, but I knew that everyone in the city was either angry or past caring. All had lost both family members and friends in this horrific war and were looking for someone to blame.

"When God first called me to be a prophet," I said, "I used to pray for the nation, but many years ago God forbade me from doing so anymore. What would you do?"

"Oh, I don't know," he said irritably. "You know that no-one in my family has ever claimed to be a prophet. We are administrators, advisors, sometimes even leaders." He stopped for a moment and looked at me intently. "You know, Jeremiah, my father Ahikam, my grandfather Shaphan, and his father before him, all of us have had to do our best to straighten out the messes that others keep landing us in. Particularly when it comes to religion. Being God's chosen people doesn't seem to have helped any of us much."

"We have always wanted everything our own way, not God's way. We promise to obey, but then do whatever we want instead."

"Led by the priests!"

"Often, yes. And the kings. And the officials. And the prophets. With all the people eager to follow."

"Yes, I know. But now that the worst is over, what do we do?"

I distinctly remember those words and his assumption that things could only get better after such a disaster. Yet he was wrong: there was still worse to come, although we didn't know it at that time. At that stage, Gedaliah assumed that his job as governor in Jerusalem would be to rebuild Judah as a subject nation under much stricter Chaldean supervision. If only that had been all.

The rest of our conversation isn't worth reporting. I felt the need to justify my behaviour, a reaction that I have done my best to avoid throughout my career. God told me that I should be like an immovable wall standing against the nation, and a wall does not try to justify why it stands where it does.

ℚℛ

Gedaliah and his limited staff were trying to make Jerusalem liveable again. It was a massive job. Eighteen uninterrupted months of an aggressive siege had brought the city to the brink of starvation, and the final defeat had come with a deluge of death.

What a monumental task Gedaliah had accepted! He must take control over the recovery from a catastrophe that almost defied description. Bodies still lay on every street. Food supplies were basically non-existent and the water supplies were mostly corrupted. Uninjured citizens were helping the injured as best they could, but many were simply too weak to recover. His dedication inspired my admiration and I knew that he would do his best – but I did not envy him the responsibility.

One morning I went out into the city briefly to see what had happened since the city was overthrown. The overpowering stench of rotting flesh caused my stomach to revolt and I only just avoided vomiting. The earlier attempt to remove the bodies had failed when many of the Judeans pressed into service had proved too weak to move the corpses. People reported in tones of wide-eyed horror the scene that had greeted their eyes on the morning after the city fell. Many of the stacked bodies had no longer been complete. To be sure, birds had been attacking the bodies, but birds do not use knives to hack off limbs. Dead bodies, even the emaciated bodies of relatives and friends, had helped to satisfy the desperate hunger of the starving survivors.

After a week, however, the bodies were in such a state of decay that not even the desperation of hunger could drive people to approach them. The stench seemed to grab my stomach and squeeze. It was hard even to force myself to breathe.

Three days later, the Chaldeans arranged for some food to be brought into the city. Rumours spread like wildfire and thousands gathered around the gates in barely-contained desperation. Chaldean soldiers threw bread into the crowds like a householder throwing scraps to his dogs. Many of those who shared in the limited bounty were herded into compounds outside the city and branded. These may have been the fortunate ones, as they were to be fed so that they could be used for the work required around the city. But though they were able to eat, they also had to endure the unspeakable horror of moving the thousands of rotting corpses that were scattered across the city out into the Valley of the Son of Hinnom, where they fed the rekindled fires for which that valley was famous. Yet now, it was not religious perversion that initiated the conflagration, but sheer irresistible necessity. The rotting dead must be disposed of, and the number of corpses made burial impossible. Fire was the only answer, and even that was difficult. Wood is always in high demand during a siege, and few trees remained within walking distance of Jerusalem. Instead, many houses were torn down to provide the wood needed to consume what remained of the dead once they were dumped in the Valley of Slaughter.

Birds and wild animals helped, of course. They feasted on the remains of the men, women and children of Judah, just as God had promised.[52]

❧

Three weeks had passed since the ninth day of the fourth month when the city had fallen. A new month had begun, and slowly Jerusalem was returning to something closer to normal. The streets had been cleared of the detritus of war and about half of the buildings that had collapsed over them. Most of the dead bodies had been cleared away, and the living had access to food once more – although often at a very high price which put it beyond the reach of the poor.

I certainly don't want to make it sound as if there were no problems. Chaldean soldiers still surrounded Jerusalem and continued to work their way through the city, ransacking the empty houses and seeing what they could find in the houses with living inhabitants. Resistance was futile and often fatal – as the citizens should have known already from previous experiences with the Chaldean army.

We heard very little news from outside the city and knew nothing about what had happened in the countryside since Jerusalem had fallen.

Zedekiah was a prisoner of King Nebuchadnezzar, that much we knew – but it had been almost a month since his failed attempt to escape from the city under cover of darkness. There are always people who are willing to speak confidently in such situations, and many were sure

---

[52] Jeremiah 7:33; 16:4; 19:7; 34:20

that Zedekiah would be executed by King Nebuchadnezzar. Others hoped that Yahweh might protect him and give him another chance to escape!

I knew that he would meet King Nebuchadnezzar and be taken captive to Babylon. He would pay for his broken oaths and unfaithfulness in this time of final punishment. Already, his throne and crown had been taken away, and no son of his would ever rule over Judah.

But no-one wanted to hear my words on that subject – or any other. It was as if I was a man who borrowed money and never paid it back. Everyone viewed me with hatred and contempt and avoided my company as much as possible.

There were three significant exceptions to this: Ebed-melech the Ethiopian eunuch, Baruch the scribe and my mother. All were still alive, and all gave thanks to God for it. So did I.

Gedaliah was also willing to tolerate me, but he obviously questioned my actions and motives.

As the days passed, I began to reminisce as I wandered around the city with little to do.

I sat in the temple courts one afternoon, my mind filled with memories of better times. I saw in my mind's eye a platform with a young king reading from the Book of the Law, and I thought back to a time when national righteousness had actually seemed possible. Josiah had provided the leadership, and the Book of the Law the foundation to anchor it to. Worship had been a work of joy, and many thousands had answered Josiah's call to obedience.

My friends from Bethel, Shobai, Maacah and Miriam, had all given their heart to the worship of a kind and loving God. Now, all three were dead and the nation had lost its heart. What was more, no king sat on the throne, either.

I remembered a joyous night: a night of Passover celebration. Jerusalem had been ringed with campfires and happiness, while songs of praise had filled the moonlit air. Bonfires had warmed the open squares of the city also, and happy fellowship had strengthened the love that a man must feel for his neighbour.

But now, all were either taken into captivity or dead, enemies and friends alike. And the kingdom was dead also. Never again would a king sit on the throne of Judah until… until what? Yahweh had spoken to me twice of "a righteous branch" coming from the line of David to reign as king.[53] But when would he come? It could not happen until the nation had been regathered from the captivity into which God was still sending it. Yet I knew that the captivity would last for 70 years.[54]

Would he be the next king of Jerusalem? The great king?

These two messages had shown me that both this king and the city itself would be called "The Lord is our righteousness".[55]

With at least 70 years to flow in God's plan before these wonderful events could happen, I knew that I would not see them happen. For me, life would end in the middle of a captivity that had come because no-one would listen to the words of Yahweh.

Of course I had the same hope as Abraham, Isaac and Jacob, those patriarchs who had been promised a land and never yet inherited it. I know that I will see God in my flesh when he fulfils those promises, but I also know that death will take me first, as it has already taken Abraham, Isaac and Jacob.

---

[53] Jeremiah 23:5; 33:15

[54] Jeremiah 25:11-12; 29:10

[55] Jeremiah 23:6; 33:16

These were not particularly happy thoughts, although they did centre around a coming king of righteousness, but they led me to thoughts of the destruction of Jerusalem that had not come either.

Was it still to come or was this another prophecy from which God had relented?

By then, it was the ninth day of the fifth month. Exactly one month had passed since Nebuchadnezzar's army had breached the impenetrable walls of Zion. Summer was drawing to a close and a gentle breeze was blowing from the west as the afternoon wore on. It was a peaceful scene.

Suddenly I heard the sound of trumpets – a harsh sound in the distance to the north. They sounded like Chaldean trumpet calls and grew slowly louder as I listened, so I walked out of the temple towards the Benjamin Gate. The Chaldean guards at the gate allowed me to climb up to the top of the wall above the gate. They seemed to recognise me. So did the man who was sweeping the street near the gate. He spat as I walked past.

I looked out towards the Chaldean camps that still surrounded the city. It was clear that the sound was stirring some urgent movement there, and I wondered why. The trumpet sounds continued to approach, and finally a large band of horsemen came into view. Important officers were obviously among the company, and as they drew closer, I thought that I could recognise the splendid costumes of some of them. They swept into the main camp and dismounted.

For some reason, I stayed, watching as the sun sank towards the horizon, and I saw a messenger despatched to the city driving a chariot. He rode through the gate beneath me and returned a short time later with Gedaliah riding beside him in the chariot. It was evident that he had been summoned by the officers of Nebuchadnezzar, so if I wanted to hear any news, I would do best to return to our lodging and wait for him there.

A short time after darkness had fallen, Gedaliah returned with the Chaldean messenger. I was there waiting for him. His features were carefully schooled into impassiveness, but around his eyes I saw a look of shock which sent a thrill of fear through my chest. Had he heard some bad news?

"What news, Gedaliah?" I called as he climbed down from the chariot. He waited until the chariot had turned and driven off before answering.

"Come inside and I'll tell you."

We walked inside and into the room he used as an office, and I waited expectantly. "News from Riblah?" I prompted.

He looked at me suspiciously, but answered, "Yes. A little news about King Zedekiah and his men. Zedekiah will be judged very soon by King Nebuchadnezzar. In the meantime, though, they have killed all of his advisors and nobles, including those men who threw you into the cistern, Shephatiah the son of Mattan, Gedaliah the son of Pashhur, Jehucal the son of Shelemiah and Pashhur the son of Malchiah."

"They won't terrorise Ebed-melech again either," I said. "That's good."

"I think the world is better off without most of the advisors King Zedekiah chose to listen to."

"True. Well, it seems we'll still have to wait to hear exactly what Nebuchadnezzar does to Zedekiah. But I can guarantee you that he won't be killed like his advisors. Was there anything else?" I asked, trying to work out what had caused his look of shock.

"Nothing that I'm going to tell you. You'll find out soon enough."

❧

The next day I found out what Gedaliah meant: it was just what I had feared.

On the tenth day of the fifth month, the Chaldeans burned Jerusalem with fire. Obviously there had been a change of plan so that Jerusalem was not to be revived after all.

It was no surprise to me that their change of plan had caused the prophecies of Yahweh to be fulfilled. No doubt the Chaldean king or his officers thought they had sound reasons for their decisions. But whatever they thought and whatever their plans may have been, it was God's plan that came through.

Flames leapt from the roof of the great temple of Solomon. Priceless carved wooden panelling fuelled the fire.

The palace of the kings of Judah was likewise wreathed in flame, and embers soared into the night air before settling elsewhere to spread the hungry flames across the city.

Strong, swirling winds fanned the flames, spreading their clutching fingers from building to building until fires were spread across the length and breadth of the city and a massive, rolling, pall of blinding smoke blanketed the city – a pall that was periodically thinned, but never cleared, by the temperamental winds.

Wood and wool, skins and linen, papyrus and hair, foodstuffs and flesh, all fed the fires of Jerusalem as God poured out his final judgement on the city.

Though overwhelming in their murky, billowing blackness during the day, the fires were, nevertheless, strangely beautiful at night.

No attempt was made to put out the flames.

As the intensity reduced over the following days, the fire was almost like a living thing feeding on the city's buildings – nibbling, grazing, making sure that nothing was missed. The fires consumed every important building, and as they burned, Nebuchadnezzar's army systematically reduced all of Jerusalem's massive walls to rubble.

Jerusalem, the city of peace, was no more.

Chapter 10

Demolition

I had seen the destruction of the city first hand. It was a massive task carefully executed by experts. Cautiously, I had made sure that I did not get too close to the Chaldean soldiers who were setting fires and promoting their spread. The men were a rough, loud, arbitrary and violent lot, the sort who might decide at any moment that one of the flaming houses would make a good pyre for a watching Israelite who they thought had looked at them in the wrong way.

From a distance, therefore, I had watched, horrified, as soldiers began to methodically demolish the temple.

They started by emptying the temple storerooms, stacking countless items in piles as I might have set up so many large bonfires. The supervising officers seemed to know exactly what they were trying to achieve and gave their men very specific orders. A grim thought occurred to me – if you conquer and burn enough cities, you must develop quite a skill for setting fires!

It hurt to watch as ancient scrolls were stacked alongside painted idols and carved lucky charms ready to be burned – the precious with the worthless. Most of the items of gold and silver had already been collected together and taken outside the city to Nebuchadnezzar's camps, but from time to time, additional treasures were found and waved about exultantly before they too began their journey to the ever-growing treasuries of Nebuchadnezzar in Babylon.

I saw a group of men gathered around the base of each of the two massive bronze columns that stood outside the nave of the temple. Sledgehammers rose and fell methodically, each stroke making a deep and echoing thud. From a distance, I could not see clearly what they were doing, but I guessed that they were trying to weaken the foundations under the enormous columns, with the intention of making them fall. Jachin and Boaz, they were called, and it took three tall men, stretched fingertip to fingertip, to reach around the circumference of either. They towered above the pavement, each crowned with a lily-shaped capital and decorated with a bronze network and many pomegranates.

The majestic edifice had been my family's workplace for almost 400 years, ever since Solomon had dedicated it to Yahweh, the God of Israel. It was not made of flimsy materials. But the temple was no longer the house of God, and it was tragic to think of the changes that had taken place since it was first dedicated exclusively to Yahweh.

King David, probably the greatest king ever to rule over Israel, had wanted to build a temple to Yahweh, but Yahweh had told him that he could not do so because he had killed too many people, and waged great wars.[56] Instead, God's house would be built by David's son Solomon, who would be a man of peace. Yet David had been desperately eager to collect materials that could be used to build the house of the God he loved so deeply. During the rest of his life, he had amassed vast quantities of gold, silver, bronze, iron, wood and stone for the project[57] and he had also directed Solomon to gather even more. David had been determined that the temple should be magnificent beyond anything that anyone could yet imagine, just as the God he worshipped was so far above all other so-called gods.

David's love for Yahweh comes through so clearly in both the Psalms he wrote and the way he lived. He inspired a generation of Israelites, along with a large number of foreigners, to worship Yahweh with a purity and sincerity that has never been matched since in the history of my nation. Yet David died without seeing the temple – except in his imagination. He left behind a nation hungry for the worship of Yahweh and yearning for a temple in which their worship could see fuller expression.

Four years had passed as Solomon finished making preparations, then the nation had waited seven more years as the temple had gradually grown on Mount Moriah. Massive stones had been painstakingly shaped off-site before being brought to the site for assembly. Eyes both inside and outside the city had watched eagerly as the temple had begun to command the skyline of Jerusalem. Tawny walls and pavements had demanded their attention, and visitors had started with surprise when they saw its progress for the first time.

---

[56] 1 Chronicles 22:8
[57] 1 Chronicles 22:14

As the temple neared completion, Jerusalem was becoming more than a city of peace, it was becoming the city of God – and the nation waited with bated breath. A love for God filled the heart of the nation and worship longed for a fuller expression in this new house of holiness.

Finally it was finished, and hundreds of thousands of people, possibly even millions – it was hard to be sure from the eyewitness accounts – gathered for the dedication of the temple. Solomon's planning had made sure that everything was ready, and the huge crowd watched in awe as their king knelt humbly on a platform and spread out his hands towards heaven.

It was a seminal moment.

The splendid mix of love and fear that Yahweh had demanded from his people at Mount Sinai was now living in their hearts on Mount Moriah. Their king led the nation in prayer, expressing their utter dependence on God and their craving for his presence in their midst. No heart was untouched by the honest acknowledgement of sin and a desire to do better – to obey more completely.

Solomon's prayer traversed the widely different situations that can occupy the life of a nation, times of hope and happiness, disaster and terror – and in its supreme phrases the crowd revelled in a unity of worship they had never even imagined before.

The prayer ended and the crowd collectively took a deep breath and marvelled at how closely a nation could be bound together. Suddenly, fire came down from heaven – all of the accounts I had found agreed on this – and consumed the burnt offering and the sacrifices that had been prepared. A gasp of surprise and fear spread through the temple courts, the nearby streets and even the hillside opposite where crowds stood on the Mount of Olives. Wherever they stood, they fell to their knees, then bowed to the ground, filled with a fear that inspired thankfulness to Yahweh, the God who had chosen Israel.

My ancestors, the priests, had been unable to enter the new house of Yahweh because the glory of Yahweh had filled his house.

It was a superlative moment.

Israel was utterly dedicated to her God. For a moment – and maybe only a moment – true love and dedication filled the nation, and nobody could doubt the visible confirmation that Yahweh had accepted them.

But time moves on.

Once again, daily life took pride of place in the planning of the nation. The heavenly conflagration was not completely forgotten, but its importance lessened.

We fall from the heights of holiness so quickly.

Even King Solomon the Wise was distracted – he concentrated on gold and silver, on women and their whims, and on his own desires. His descendants had followed his lead, except for a very few who, like Josiah, had genuinely sought to walk with the God of Israel all the days of their life.

Three hundred and seventy years later, there was nothing left of the love my people had felt for Yahweh. Instead of the fire of God's affirmation, it was now the fire of God's judgement that was burning in the temple. Burning. Devouring. Spreading.

CଃR

Fires continued to spread across the city. I had expected nothing different, but I felt the loss deeply when I saw my own house burning. It seemed to be a symbol of the utter destruction of my nation. For a time, it was as if there was nothing left in the world. Even the soldiers, God's angels of destruction, had moved on to continue their work elsewhere, leaving those who suffered to their mourning.

As I stood and watched my home burn, the flames seemed to dance, but not with joy. The embers sometimes floated down around me and sometimes blew away on the strong winds as I grieved for my nation, for my family and for myself. A neighbour, who had been watching his own house being consumed by fire, came across and spoke to me.

"This is your fault, Jeremiah," he said, accusingly.

"No," I answered, shaking my head and sighing, "this is what we have all chosen."

"I didn't choose this!" he answered angrily.

"In Moses' day, God put before our fathers the choice between life and death. Life, if we loved him, worshipped him and obeyed his commandments. Death, if we worshipped other gods and did not obey God's commandments."[58]

"But I worshipped Yahweh. I went to the temple. At times I even kept the feasts."

"And what about that shrine in your house? The shrine of Baal? What about your son whom you offered to Molech? As a nation, we have chosen the path that God said was the path of death, and now we are receiving the wages we have earned."

"But the priests told me that my worship of Yahweh was good," he argued.

"They were lying to you. And you knew it, too."

"And all the prophets – except you, that is – told me that Yahweh would keep us safe. He didn't. I don't know why I bothered worshipping him at all."

"You chose to listen to the people who said what you *wanted* to hear. I'm not the only prophet who has warned

---

[58] Deuteronomy 30:15-20

of this. God's prophets have been warning the nation of this for hundreds of years, but *no-one wanted to listen.*"

"Zedekiah, our king, led us in rebelling against Nebuchadnezzar. He told us that the Chaldeans would be too busy to bother about us and that Egypt would protect us."

"He was wrong – and you knew that God had told him so. You knew that God had warned him."

"You've always hated us, haven't you? My wife and my oldest son are both dead. The Chaldeans killed them on the day when the city fell. I suppose you're glad that so many people are dead!"

"No, I'm not glad, my friend – I'm devastated. For 40 years I've done my best to convince everyone to change, but I've failed."

"But you spent all of your time telling us that we were going to be destroyed whatever we did!"

As we argued, the roof of my neighbour's house collapsed and we had to step aside quickly to avoid a fierce shower of sparks that flew towards us. I put my hand on my neighbour's arm to console him, but he pushed it angrily away.

"Leave me alone!" he almost shouted. Tears were running down his face.

I turned away in despair and looked back at my own house. Its windows belched flame and the ominous sounds from the roof suggested that its own collapse was not far away.

Leaving the remains of his home, my neighbour walked aimlessly away down the street, and soon I saw him being detained by a group of soldiers who were carrying some newly-discovered loot. No doubt he would be forced to carry the goods out to the Chaldean camp. What would happen to him after that I had no way of knowing for sure, but I knew that thousands were being rounded up as the fires burned and taken outside the city to enclosures in preparation for exile.

I couldn't help thinking back to the time, several years earlier, when all Jewish slaves had been freed by rich men like my neighbour, but then, soon after, forced back into slavery. God had warned at the time that the oath-breakers would be punished with the sword, pestilence, famine and fire.[59] Wearily I acknowledged that it was all coming true, word by word. There truly was terror on every side for the people of Judah.

With a sudden crack, the ridge beam of my house surrendered to the devouring greed of the flames and fell inward. A terrifying, billowing surge of flame poured out through the doorway, narrowly missing me. Then, slowly, the front wall toppled outwards, leaving my home a flaming ruin.

❦

Later in the day, I returned to the temple, drawn almost irresistibly to the ruin of what had once been so fair. Parts of it were burning fiercely, dark smoke rising to join the thick pall of smoke that covered the city like a blanket. In other parts, soldiers were still working to set fires or demolish any standing stonework. I kept well out of their way.

Already, piles of blackened rubble had replaced many of the elegant buildings that filled my childhood memories of the temple.

At the front of the vestibule, the engineers and stone masons clustered around the bronze columns were still working hard. Since the columns stood on a raised platform, their foundations could be attacked by shattering the stonework of the platform, working inwards

---

[59] Jeremiah 34:17-22

from the smoothly finished vertical faces that jutted out into the courtyard. Now, instead of smoothly finished corners with vertical faces, there were pock-marks and jagged edges, while scattered fragments lay spread around.

Every possible angle of those corners had been tested, and it was a testament to the enduring quality of the workmanship of Solomon's stonemasons that such a wide-ranging assault was required. Progress, however, was not equal on the two corners: the foundation of Jachin, the pillar on the south, was significantly more damaged than that of its twin, Boaz. A hole was clearly visible under Jachin's base where an entire stone had been prised loose from the southern corner of the platform. Men were working busily in the void that was left, the sound of hammers ringing above the other noises of destruction, and it seemed that the two groups were having a competition as to which could topple their column first. I was glad it wasn't me doing the work, as I would have been terrified that the column would fall and crush me. But these workmen appeared confident that they were safe in their burrowing. The pace of the work was rapid, and as I watched a cheer rose from the group working near Boaz as they loosened the huge stone that matched the stone missing from under Jachin. Wedges and levers helped to remove this stone also, and the work went on with renewed vigour.

Competition was fierce, however, and by this time the crew working on Jachin had sensed that another massive stone was loosening, and were hammering in more wedges to open up the gap between it and the rest of the platform. This would take away almost half of the foundation that supported the huge bronze column. If only they could begin to tilt the column – just a little – towards the void beneath, its massive weight would no longer be working to keep it stable on its base, but would begin to help the destroyers.

Still, the work was not easy, and it took a considerable time before the block beneath Jachin was finally levered out. Yet cheers again came from the crew working on Boaz, for they had loosened the matching stone and removed it with much less difficulty than their competitors.

The contest seemed close to an end, and large groups of soldiers were urgently called on to assist. Large coils of thick rope lay on drums that sat on carts near the columns. Now was the time to use them. A lithe young man approached Jachin carrying a curved hook attached to a thinner rope. Holding the rope a short distance from the hook, he swung it effortlessly, much as a skilled slinger would make ready to cast his stone, then let go, allowing the hook to fly upwards towards the capital and the network of bronze that decorated the top of the column. The hook struck the network a glancing blow and fell back again, where it was caught deftly. Once again the rope was swung and the hook carried the rope up towards the top of the column. This time, the hook reached the top of the curved capital and hooked itself in place. Sharp tugs on the rope must have convinced the man that he could rely on the purchase he had gained, because, effortlessly, and with amazing speed, he began to climb the rope until he reached the hook. Somehow, he managed to ease himself up past the hook on to the top of the capital. Next, the end of the light rope by which the climber had ascended so easily was tied to one of the thicker, heavy ropes and pulled up to the top of the column. Swiftly, this strong rope was tied firmly to the top of the column, and then the lithe young man slid back down his thin rope. In an amazingly short time he had accomplished a task that I doubted I could have achieved at all, however long I had tried!

The attempts to drive wedges under the western side of Jachin had ceased while the young man had scaled the column, but now that he was safely down, they began again in earnest.

A similar scene was being played out with Boaz as the supervisor urged his men on. This second climber, however, saw an opportunity for glory and urged those driving in the wedges to continue even as he climbed the column. His courage was almost rewarded with death. He was standing atop the column when suddenly it lurched forward as a wedge slipped further under the column, forcing it to lean further outwards toward oblivion. The watchers gasped as the man clutched desperately at the capital, and the column wavered a little before settling down once more into stolid, unyielding rigidity.

The climber who had so narrowly escaped death shouted something unintelligible and waved his fists in the air before quickly fixing the heavier rope in place and slipping back to the ground. A risk had been taken, an advantage gained. The team assaulting Boaz seemed to be surging to victory.

Now, slaves were urged to pull the carts into place, unrolling the thick ropes ready for the soldiers who were quickly assembling in two large groups. Thirty or forty soldiers were clustered at the end of each rope as the slaves finished unrolling them.

Orders were shouted and within moments, the ropes were stretched taut and shouting soldiers were pulling the ropes in unison. The rope that was to urge Jachin towards destruction was the first to pull with a coordinated urgency, but that first tug seemed to have little impact: the column barely moved. Another order and the load was relaxed before being applied again. Pull, relax; pull, relax: on and off went the load as the officer did his best to build a rhythm that could unseat the stubborn column. Slowly, it started to rock backwards and forwards. Ever so slowly, the size of the movement seemed to increase, and as it did so, the stonemasons worked frantically with drills and sledgehammers to achieve that last, trifling – but critical – scrap of damage that would undermine the column enough to allow the straining soldiers to pull it off its foundation and topple it to the pavement. A sudden cracking movement underneath Jachin led the engineers to imagine that victory was within their grasp. A shout arose as the column tilted a little further toward the vestibule as the foundation crumbled slightly. One more pull, they thought, would surely bring that vast mass of bronze crashing to the ground! But no, the soldiers pulled to no avail as the column settled again, now with a discernible lean back towards the vestibule! The damage that had seemed to presage victory had instead given the column a greater stability – at least for the present.

Meanwhile Boaz was also swaying backwards and forwards, the soldiers straining with every pull, and their officer shouting the instructions he hoped would best match the speed with which Boaz swayed to the application of a tug that would force it over the invisible line that separated balance from instability; safety from destruction.

With each tug it seemed that Boaz must pass that point of no return, but each time, the officer had to finally shout, "Relax!" and watch as the column slowly leaned back towards the vestibule once more. Then, suddenly, as the column once again reached its further extent, ready to move away from the vestibule, the officer shouted, "One last time, boys! Pull! Pull! Pull!"

The soldiers pulled as they had never pulled before, and slowly, almost imperceptibly – so slowly that it seemed to have stopped completely – Boaz silently passed the point of no return. One of the soldiers straining at the rope sensed the victory and shouted – a frenzied, animal sound of triumph.

Quickly, then, others felt it too, and shouts rose from a hundred throats as Boaz, freed at last from a centuries-old equilibrium that had kept it standing immovable, began to fall with terrifying speed.

With a booming, shattering crash, Boaz slipped off the platform and struck the pavement of the court. Dust and showers of stone splinters filled the air, and when the dust cleared, Boaz lay, full length on the ground, split into four main pieces, though many other fragments littered the ground. Several soldiers had been injured by the shards of stone and fragments of shattered bronze. Boaz had inflicted more injuries on Chaldean soldiers in its destruction than anything else had done since the day the city fell!

Quick thinking on the part of the Chaldean engineers stopped the broken pieces of the column from rolling away across the pavement, sloped gently as it was for drainage. Heavy blocks of wood were dragged swiftly into place against each section, and the drama was over for the time being.

The engineers, stonemasons and soldiers who had toppled Boaz celebrated their victory and rejoiced over their defeated comrades.

Before long, however, Jachin too lay in pieces on the temple pavement, and the soldiers rejoiced again. Booty put money in the royal coffers. That led to a happy king, and happy soldiers – soldiers who were well paid.

Yahweh's temple was no longer the place of serene holiness that King David had imagined. Instead, it had become a profane and unholy place – a burden to God. A sanctuary profaned. A dwelling place discarded.

Foreigners had made its destruction a game, competing over the ravaging of holy items in their unceasing quest for precious materials. But by that time, nothing in the temple was holy any more. The God who made the temple holy had left.

Chapter 11

Arrested

I was walking through the city seeing what remained. Gedaliah had been warned of the coming destruction and had moved his headquarters out of the city as the fires were starting. My mother and I had left with him and temporarily relocated to a camp outside the city, but I had felt the need to return to the city briefly to witness the events I had waited so long to see. Mixed feelings were inevitable, I suppose. So many people had ridiculed my reporting of God's predictions that it was impossible not to feel some satisfaction in seeing them come true. Yet the sadness of seeing the city of my fathers go up in flames was profound. It was an empty, unpleasant victory.

"You, there!" The shout came from behind, but I ignored it.

Another voice shouted, louder this time, "Are you deaf, old man?"

I ignored that, too. I didn't feel like an old man! Since I had been able to eat again, and been free to walk around, I was feeling younger than I had for years, despite the sadness caused by recent events.

I heard running footsteps behind me and turned to see four Chaldean soldiers hurrying toward me with swords drawn and spears ready. Clearly those shouts *had* been directed at me!

"You old fool," snarled the leading runner as he approached me, "are you deaf?" His sword was pointed at me and he seemed just about to use it.

"No," I said apologetically in Aramaic, "I'm sorry. I was thinking."

"If you ignore instructions you won't be *thinking* for long," he said threateningly, though he seemed slightly mollified by my use of Aramaic as he answered in kind. "What are you doing here? We rounded up every last person in this area earlier this morning."

"I have been walking all around the city...."

"Well, you shouldn't have been. Come with us."

I started to object, but their expressions discouraged me from continuing. As I moved away with them, one of the soldiers slipped a knotted loop of rope over my head and tugged it to make sure it was sitting down properly around my neck.

"I have been given freedom to walk around the city," I protested.

"Oh, yes? By King Nebuchadnezzar himself, I suppose!" he said, sarcastically. He tugged the rope again so that I wouldn't forget what it meant, and continued, "*Nobody* has been given that freedom. Jerusalem has been burned down and we're clearing everyone out. And I mean everyone."

"But I was given freedom in the city."

"Times have changed. Once the bosses decided to destroy the city, there was no more freedom here. I'm glad they let us destroy it."

I argued and insisted with all of the stubbornness that God had instilled in me, but it made no difference. The soldiers refused to listen, and finally threatened to kill me if I would not keep quiet and cooperate. I shut up.

They led me up to the north of the city where we met others who must have been rounded up by these same soldiers. Ropes around their necks held the captives together and my rope was quickly tied to the end of the line.

Together we were led out of the city towards a compound where prisoners were being collected. The soldiers were impatient with any delay or resistance, and resorted to violence as if it were second nature to them. I cooperated and was left alone. They seemed to be tired of trying to communicate, by means of either their poor Hebrew or our awkward Aramaic, and wouldn't let us talk. However, I was confident that I would soon meet a more senior officer to whom I could explain my situation and quickly return to Gedaliah's protection.

As we approached the compound, a group of about two hundred prisoners was being led out, chained around their necks to form several long lines.

"Here are some more, Alamu," shouted the leader of our group.

"You took your time, didn't you? You almost missed us – we're just leaving. Well, grab some chains for them, Balasu, and we'll take them too."

"I need to talk to…" I began, but that was as far as I got before I was struck across the back by one of the soldiers.

"Silence," he shouted at me, as I stumbled forward, kept upright only by the rope around my neck.

For a moment I considered speaking anyway, shouting out to the officers I could see standing near the entrance of the compound, but the threatening look on the soldier's face made me decide not to.

Some soldiers hurriedly brought out chains with neck irons and we were quickly added to the lines. The chains were heavy and uncomfortable, making movement difficult.

Where were we heading? I had no idea, and the Chaldean soldiers showed no inclination to tell us. Instead, our new overseers made it clear that we were to march exactly when, where and how they directed us to – all in complete silence – or suffer the consequences. We obeyed their commands.

Marching north on the road to Bethel, I wondered, in sudden terror, whether we were setting off immediately to walk into exile to Babylon. Yet surely there would be more preparation for such a journey than that, and surely there should be more protection than the few soldiers we had with us.

As we marched, this fear marched every step beside me, until finally I decided that worrying would make no difference to the outcome and tried to calm down. It was a wise decision, but the thoughts with which I then filled my mind were far from wise.

I spent the time feeling sorry for myself and criticising God for my suffering. Ever since that night of my seventeenth birthday, I had done my best to follow God's instructions, and had been mostly content with his appointment of me as a prophet. But on the road to Ramah that day, I wanted to quit.

God's work had brought me nothing but trouble, I told myself, and I dwelt on all the trouble I could think of. Certainly forty years of prophesying to an unheeding nation meant that I had plenty of examples to mull over.

I suppose that the only really wise thing I did was to decide that I should not pray "formally" to God about this until I had had some time to compose myself in private. However, having made this choice, I then felt free to complain as the fancy took me.

I won't list all the complaints I compiled on that long afternoon. I am ashamed of it now, and it was never going to be helpful in any way, given how utterly self-centred it was.

We walked on throughout that long, hot afternoon. The column did not move quickly because we were all still learning how to walk with an unyielding metal collar around our neck, joined to others by heavy chains. Beatings were common as people stumbled or tripped, crying out with pain and often upsetting the balance of the prisoners on either side of them. I was very careful to remain silent and equally careful to avoid tripping, but it was difficult. In the end, the only time I was beaten was when the man two in front of me slipped as a stone moved under his feet, which upset the balance of the man in front of me, who fell and dragged me down with him. Fortunately, I was at the end of the line, so my fall affected no-one behind me, but the three of us who had stumbled or fallen were each beaten with many hard strokes of a cane.

After about two hours of walking, we turned off onto a side road which I knew led to Ramah. I heaved a sigh of relief that we weren't continuing north immediately, and walked on with a little more hope.

As we climbed the rise to Ramah we saw that an enclosure with tall stone walls had been constructed on the hillside. Through a gap in the wall, crowds of people could be seen inside and we were marched up to the gap to meet a group of Chaldean soldiers who were on guard.

"More prisoners from Jerusalem," called the soldier at the front of our column.

"Take 'em in," replied the officer.

"Alright. And here's the docket for them."

The officer scanned the sheet he was given and said, "So we don't even get names now. How many more are there to come?"

"We're down to the last few, I think. This lot could even be the last large bunch."

"Ah, so these are the dregs," said the officer, smiling a little.

"Yes, sir, they look like dregs, don't you think?"

"The whole nation looks like dregs to me."

"Well then, these must be the dregs of the dregs."

All of this was in Aramaic, and only a few in the column seemed to understand the laughs of the soldiers at our expense.

Despite the laughs, though, there was no lessening of either the strict requirement for silence, or the cruelty with which we were driven in through the entrance.

Once we were inside the compound, I waited for the chains to be removed, but they weren't. I found later that all of the Judeans within the walls were chained together in groups, and in those groups they must stay for everything. Groups were taken out for toileting once per day, and if people could not wait, they must do their business where they sat. Summer was coming to an end, but it was still hot weather, and the compound stank.

As we looked for a place in the compound where we could sit down and rest, the members of my group looked around for people they knew. I looked around too and tried to estimate how many people the compound held. At first, I thought it must be several hundred, but as I counted the knots of people and added them together, I began to see that the number must be much larger – thousands at least.

I saw quite a few people that I recognised, but none whom I would have called friends, and none gave any sort of greeting. It seemed to be me against the world, as usual.

Others were able to find friends, however, and we ended up in a rather crowded position near three groups that each contained a few friends of various members of my group. As we settled down, several recognised me and suggested that I should go somewhere else. I don't know how they thought that I could do so! The suggestions were made in quiet, but audible, voices. Apparently the Chaldeans here were willing to allow us to speak, and my hopes rose again. Maybe I could find some way of getting the attention of a Chaldean officer who would actually listen to my story. But how would my countrymen respond when they saw that I wanted to speak to a Chaldean soldier? They already considered me a coward or a traitor – or both – and I might be in real danger if they knew what I planned to do. Why had God allowed this to happen to me?

By this time it was getting late in the afternoon and the sun was setting, so I kept quiet and slept under the stars that night with the rest of the captives. As I lay amongst them and looked up at the night sky I wondered, was I really one of them – a captive being taken into exile – or a quisling whose foreign masters had abandoned him?

℞

The next morning dawned bright and clear. The cool brought about little improvement in the smell in the compound, and the abundant dew had made everything wet, as usual.

By mid-morning I was still unsure what to do. I was hoping that when we were called for our toilet opportunity I would be able to talk to a soldier and see what I could achieve. I knew it would be dangerous, but I couldn't think of any better ideas.

I had made sure that I was always facing towards the gate of the compound, watching for any opportunity that might arise. As noon approached, I saw several chariots and a crowd of horsemen arrive at the gate. Some obviously important officials climbed down from the chariots and spoke to the guards at the gate. They seemed to be asking questions, and did not look very happy with the answers they were receiving. It was too far away for me to see or hear very clearly what was going on, but I could still hear raised voices and see waving arms. Then some soldiers came into the compound and began to make their way around, past different groups of captives, asking questions. After a while, the soldiers began to look in our direction and finally made their way towards our group.

"Is Jeremiah, the son of Hilkiah, here?" I heard them ask a group some distance from us.

"You mean Jeremiah the traitor?" came a deliberately loud response.

"Jeremiah the traitor!" called another voice, and soon many more joined in.

"Traitor, traitor, traitor," they all shouted, including the man right next to me.

"I'm here," I yelled, as loudly as I could, but my voice was drowned out by the many that condemned me.

Then another man standing near me decided to do more than just shout, and within moments I was being punched and kicked by as many others as could reach me. Fortunately, the Chaldean soldiers saw the disturbance and hurried over, using their canes freely to stop the attack on me. One of their swings hit me too, but without their intervention I doubt that I would have survived for long. Heavy chains can be dangerous weapons.

When the melee was quieted and reinforcements had arrived, armed with swords and spears rather than just canes, the soldiers asked me who I was.

After confirming my identity, they freed me from the chain around my neck, chained my hands instead and led me out of the compound to where the officers were waiting. There were no buildings on the site and the soldiers seemed to live in small tents into which they were loth to invite their senior officers, so I saw a cluster of chairs on which several senior Chaldean officers were seated. One I recognised with relief as Nebuzaradan, the captain of Nebuchadnezzar's guard.

I was led forward and pushed down onto my knees before him. I could tell that he had recognised me, and realised with surprise that he looked pleased to see me. No doubt he had been a little concerned over losing a prisoner whom the king had told him to look after! However, I was to find that his care was more than just a concern for his own career.

"Ah, Jeremiah," said Nebuzaradan as he sat, sipping a drink. Then he looked at me more closely, and I saw genuine distress in his eyes. "You don't look well. What happened?"

I didn't feel well either. The beating I had received from the Chaldeans on the way to Ramah, followed by the savage attack by my own countrymen in the last few minutes, had left me badly bruised and in considerable pain.

"While I was walking around Jerusalem, as you said I could, I was detained by Chaldean soldiers," I said bitterly, a swollen lip slurring my speech. I was beyond caring what might happen to me for speaking like that to such a senior officer among our conquerors. "They wouldn't listen to me and dragged me here, beating me on the way. Here, they still wouldn't listen and…."

"Well, Jeremiah," Nebuzaradan interrupted smoothly, "we're sorry that this has happened. It should never have done so and we will do our best to make up for your suffering – although in this sort of war, I'm afraid that everyone suffers. No-one is exempt. Yahweh your God pronounced this disaster against this place and he has made it happen. He has done as he said. Because you sinned against the Lord and did not obey his voice, this thing has come upon you. Now, see, I release you today from the chains on your hands."

As he spoke, he beckoned to a soldier who came and released the chains from my hands. I stood up and the soldier looked questioningly at Nebuzaradan, who seemed to silently confirm that it was alright for me to stand instead of kneeling.

"If it seems good to you to come with me to Babylon," Nebuzaradan continued, "come, and I will look after you well, but if it seems wrong to you to come with me to Babylon, do not come."

My distaste for the former suggestion must have shown in my face, for Nebuzaradan smiled and continued, "It's not such a bad place, Jeremiah. Its massive walls have a grandeur that Jerusalem has never equalled. Broad avenues, delightful parks, elegant buildings – but never mind, you don't have to go there. You can stay in Judah. See, the whole land is before you; go wherever you think it good and right to go."

"Is it safe for me to go anywhere? Chaldean soldiers will take me prisoner, and my own people want to kill me!"

"If you remain, then return to Gedaliah the son of Ahikam, son of Shaphan, whom the king of Babylon appointed governor of the cities of Judah, and dwell with him among the people. He will protect you."

"You mean go back to Jerusalem?"

"No, not Jerusalem. Today Gedaliah has moved to Mizpah. Jerusalem is a ruin. No-one can live there anymore. The temple lies in ashes and the walls of the city in ruins. Only a few of the poorest of the people will remain in the land, and I will be giving them vineyards and farms to care for, spreading them over many parts of the land. Jerusalem has no future. Go to Gedaliah in Mizpah, or go wherever you think it right to go."

We spoke for a few more minutes, and Nebuzaradan showed a genuine interest in what I would do. But though he pressed me to decide, I hadn't yet made up my mind, and didn't want to do so until I had prayed about it.

That was the best decision I had made for quite some time. Finally, as a prophet of God, I had decided to let God decide what I should do. As it turned out, I had almost left it too late.

Nebuzaradan gave orders and soon a large, heavy-looking bag was brought and given to him.

"Jeremiah," he said, opening the bag and showing me the contents, "here is some food for you. It should be enough to allow you to travel anywhere in the land, plus a little more to keep you fed until you can arrange food for yourself. There is also a bag of silver as a present. I hope that it will cover any costs that you may have and help you to feel a little better about the undeserved suffering that you have endured. There is also a letter from me granting you freedom, including the freedom to move anywhere throughout Judah. Take care of it."

He smiled again and handed me the bag. I was free to go.

But where should I go?

I walked thoughtfully away from the compound and past the town of Ramah. There I found a hillside that reminded me strongly of my favourite hillside outside Anathoth. Sometime, I thought, I would have to return to Anathoth to see what remained there. Had the Chaldeans destroyed it as God's prophecies suggested they might? I hoped so, because I was sure that the inhabitants deserved it. I fell to thinking about all the plots that had been made against me – at least the ones that I knew about – including the most recent attempt to kill me that afternoon in the compound. My friends hated me, my family hated me, all of my countrymen hated me. Only my mother would stand by me, and it seemed so unfair for her.

Woe is me, my mother, that you bore me, a man of strife and contention to the whole land! I have not lent, nor have I borrowed, yet all of them curse me.[60]

Those were the thoughts in my mind, formed in words as my thoughts normally are, but not directed at God, although they were complaining about the consequences for me of doing his work.

Nevertheless, he answered me – but this time it was not a gentle presence that warmed, but a sharp, imperious announcement that burned within and filled me with fear:

"Have I not set you free for their good?
Have I not pleaded for you before the enemy
in the time of trouble and in the time of distress?
Can one break iron,
iron from the north, and bronze?

"Your wealth and your treasures I will give as spoil,
without price, for all your sins,
throughout all your territory.
I will make you serve your enemies

---

[60] Jeremiah 15:10

> in a land that you do not know,
> for in my anger a fire is kindled
> that shall burn forever."[61]

God had set me free. He had done it for the good of my nation, while I had been thinking only of myself. God was unquestionably judging my people, but his decisions and his processes were still well beyond my understanding and outside my control. God knew what he was doing. I did not.

Sitting there on the hillside I had more opportunity to think in undisturbed peace than I had had for at least a month. The sun was sliding down behind the hill on which I sat. Sunset was approaching. As I sat and thought, I realised just how long it had been since I had enjoyed a sunrise or sunset in the presence of God. Living in Jerusalem had made it difficult for several years, then being locked in the house of Jonathan and the court of the guard had made it completely impossible. Then when I had been freed from the court of the guard, I had been too busy. The sun had always risen and set, but I had been too pre-occupied with other things to regain my habit of prayer. No wonder I had been seeing only the problems and not God's power to give solutions! Thinking back over the past few weeks, I saw at last how far I had let myself slip away from God.

Was I still really his prophet?

---

[61] Jeremiah 15:11-14

Chapter 12

Reinstated

Sunset that night was an enchanting display of fluid, shifting colours that rolled and shimmered across the few clouds that floated above me, tracing their edges in a brilliant golden light that faded slowly to a deep sable. As the sky darkened, innumerable pinpricks of icy blue shone down and seemed to take away my worries and ease my suffering. The breathtaking beauty of the scene drew my thoughts away from the life I had been enduring since the Chaldeans had forced me to stay in Jerusalem. Life began to appear once more as something that held opportunities and value.

After what seemed like an age, I felt, at last, able to see once more the magnificence of God's power. I was reminded of just how much I had been missing by not seeking out the daily revelation of the sun in the morning and its shrouding again each evening. These glories of God's creation have always helped me to see both his boundless authority and his care for beauty, yet I had been missing out on them without caring enough to fight against it.

I felt the indescribable pleasure of drawing closer to God again, yet I knew that I still had important business to sort out. I had been complaining to God, objecting to his treatment of me and planning to present it to him in careful prayer. I no longer felt the same strength in my complaints, but I did feel that I needed to admit my condition before him. So I looked up at the stars and struggled to arrange my complaints in order as well as I could. Then I prayed: "O Lord, you know; remember me and visit me, and take vengeance for me on my persecutors. In your forbearance take me not away; know that for your sake I bear reproach. Your words were found, and I ate them, and your words became to me a joy and the delight of my heart, for I am called by your name, O Lord, God of hosts. I did not sit in the company of revellers, nor did I rejoice; I sat alone, because your hand was upon me, for you had filled me with indignation. Why is my pain unceasing, my wound incurable, refusing to be healed? Will you be to me like a deceitful brook, like waters that fail?"[62]

My prayer was not delivered in the same mood of criticism as it would have been a day earlier. Instead, there was some of the humility that should be there. Yet it was still a report of complaints. I had suffered and felt that it was unfair.

Yahweh answered me uncompromisingly:

> "If you return, I will restore you,
> and you shall stand before me.
> If you utter what is precious,

---

[62] Jeremiah 15:15-18

and not what is worthless,
you shall be as my mouth."[63]

His first words struck me like a hammer blow, and filled me with terror. *"Return."* Had my behaviour taken me away from God? Had I truly left him, left his side, left his employ? I forced myself to admit that by wallowing in self-pity and rejecting God's promised care, I had indeed done so. In that moment, I felt completely lost and utterly alone. There could have been no better way to make me realise just how much I loved God and his laws, loved his plans, loved his promises, loved his character and everything about him. Yet I had failed to hold on to him and stay by his side. I had allowed my situation to drag me down. If I accepted God's renewed offer to be his prophet, could I do any better? For me, it was a moment of proper humility in which I acknowledged my weaknesses and failures. I felt a genuine doubt about *myself*, not about God, and the mood of God's presence changed completely, to a feeling of an encircling, strengthening love as he offered me just the help I needed.

"They shall turn to you,
but you shall not turn to them.
And I will make you to this people
a fortified wall of bronze;
they will fight against you,
but they shall not prevail over you,
for I am with you
to save you and deliver you,
declares the Lord.
I will deliver you out of the hand of the wicked,
and redeem you from the grasp of the ruthless."[64]

In some ways it was like being taken back to the night of my seventeenth birthday, so many years before. God

---

[63] Jeremiah 15:19
[64] Jeremiah 15:19-21

was speaking to me and offering me a job, the opportunity to work for him as a prophet.

I seized the offer immediately. What else could I do? There was nothing else I wanted, and nothing else that could offer any hope either. God *had* always cared for me, and as I contemplated my current situation I realised that he had still continued to care for me even while I had been rebelling against him, speaking worthless things and trying to control my own destiny instead of resting in his care.

While I had remained an immovable stone in presenting God's words, he had stood with me through everything, but once I had started to look for my own way, everything had begun to seem much more difficult and the attacks of those around me had intensified. Yet even in this, God had never abandoned me. He cared for me and had now given me another chance. In fact, many more chances.

Now I had the opportunity to reset our relationship. I must again focus on delivering God's words in God's ways – and God would again make me an immovable rock among my people.

With relief I expressed my thankfulness to God and was overwhelmed by his encouraging presence filling me once more.

Despite the death and destruction that I had witnessed, everything was right once more.

❧

Night passed slowly and I alternated between periods of fitful sleep and hours of prayer. My worries were over and it was pure joy to feel that I was truly on God's side again, walking to his beat, walking in safety.

Yet there was still the knowledge that terror was indeed on every side for those of my people who had survived.   Could Gedaliah give rest to the few who remained?

Back in Jerusalem, so many had died in the pestilence and famine that had spread while the Chaldean army crouched, ready to pounce.   When they had finally pounced after 18 months of waiting, they had killed many more with the sword – the bodies left to rot or be eaten by the birds and beasts.   No-one would ever know exactly how many had died, and there would be no record of the fathers and mothers, the husbands and wives, the sons and daughters upon whom God had poured out his vengeance.   No-one would report exactly how many had been dumped in that cruel valley, cursed Topheth, now rightly called the Valley of Slaughter.   All had been left to the care of the gods in whom they had trusted, idols who could not hear or see or help.

In the compound near Ramah, many of God's people who had survived would be sleeping fitfully as I was, but without the loving arms of God around them to soothe their fears.   If only they had listened.   During the siege and even afterwards, many had asked me what was to happen to them and where they should go.   God's answer had been chilling, yet step by step it was being fulfilled:

" 'Those who are for pestilence, to pestilence,
and those who are for the sword, to the sword;
those who are for famine, to famine,
and those who are for captivity, to captivity.'
I will appoint over them four kinds of destroyers,
declares the Lord:
the sword to kill,
the dogs to tear,
and the birds of the air
and the beasts of the earth
to devour and destroy.
And I will make them a horror
to all the kingdoms of the earth

because of what Manasseh the son of Hezekiah,
king of Judah, did in Jerusalem."[65]

☙

God kept me safe from wild animals during the night, and sunrise was again a time of joyous communion with him. I watched the sun rise over the mountains of Moab and it was like being back in my early days as a prophet, in the times when I faced opposition from all around but rested safely in the support of Yahweh.

I ate some of the food that Nebuzaradan had given me, then began my journey to Mizpah. I did not want to pass Ramah and the compound of captives again, so I headed north for a while before turning west until I met the main road. After two hours of slow walking, I came to Mizpah.

It was a striking lesson. Mizpah is a small town, yet the famine, the pestilence and the massacre in Jerusalem had reduced the population so much that this small town was large enough to be the capital of Judah.

"Who are you?" asked one of the two Chaldean soldiers standing at the gate.

"I am Jeremiah, the son of Hilkiah," I replied. "I have come to join Gedaliah the son of Ahikam."

"How came you to be walking free in the land?"

"Nebuzaradan gave me leave to travel wherever I wish."

"The captain of the guard?" The voice was tinged with awe.

I smiled and answered, "Yes. I have a letter from him." I took the precious sheet of parchment from my bag and showed it to him. He read it and then looked at

---

[65] Jeremiah 15:2-4

me admiringly. "I've never even met the lord Nebuzaradan. How did you win his favour? Did you work for him as a spy?"

There it was again – more questioning of which side I was on, but I found that it worried me less now that I had been reconciled with God.

"I am a prophet of Yahweh, the God of Israel." It was good to be able to say that with confidence again. "Yahweh told the people in Jerusalem that they should surrender to King Nebuchadnezzar. Some did so and the king felt that this had helped with the final defeat of the city. He ordered that I should be looked after."

"You must be having it easy then. He doesn't always look after his soldiers that way!"

"King Nebuchadnezzar is being used to punish the people of Judah for their unfaithfulness, but his time will come too. If only he would learn to worship Yahweh himself."

"Why would anyone ever worship a losing god? We only worship winners in Babylon." He turned towards the gateway and pointed through it. "Walk through the gateway and go straight on up the hill. When you come to the biggest building in the town, that's the place where you'll find Gedaliah."

"Thanks for the advice." I took a couple of steps forward, then turned back again, saying, "You know, you'll find out soon enough that your gods aren't really winners. Idols only seem to win, but it never lasts for long. Yahweh is the living God who judges nations for their pride."

"We found more gods and idols in Jerusalem than we've ever had in Babylon!"

"Yes, but not one of them was Yahweh. Those idols are the main reason why Yahweh was punishing Judah. He is not a god whom we can define. We can't turn him into whatever we want him to be, or make images of him.

He is in control of all the nations. Almost 1,000 years ago he brought the people of Israel out of Egypt, although Pharaoh had refused to let them go at first. And in 70 years, he will bring the people of Judah back from Babylon too. None of your gods will be able to stop it. You should learn more about him and find out how to please him."

The soldier I had been speaking to was willing at least to listen to my words, but his comrade was not.

"I'm quite content with our Babylonian gods," he answered, with studied contempt. "We seem to be doing pretty well, thank you very much. Certainly much better than your people and your gods! Look at the rotting corpses everywhere – there aren't many in Chaldean uniforms."

"No, but if you don't start to acknowledge that it is Yahweh who is in control you will find yourselves on the other end of the stick when Babylon's time comes."

"Oh, cut it out," he snarled. "We'll let you in because that's what the lord Nebuzaradan wants, but be careful what you say in the town. Don't push your luck too far or one dark night you might just disappear."

He ordered me through the gates disdainfully.

As I walked through the town I found that even small Mizpah seemed rather quiet and empty. There were a few Chaldean soldiers around, but not many. There were also some men who worked for Gedaliah, but they were few indeed.

☙

"Now you make sure that you look after that wound on your arm," said my mother, fussing over me as if I were a young child again.

"Yes, mother, whatever you say, mother. I'll make sure it stays clean," I replied, laughing as I did so.

My mother smiled back at me, but still spoke in a serious voice, "You never have looked after yourself properly, young man!"

"Oh, I look after myself, but maybe this was a little bit of God leaving me to reap what I had sown. It will all get better in a day or two, but I must admit that it hurts a lot at the moment."

"I know that God told you not to get married, but sometimes I wish that you had a wife to look after you."

"I trust that God knows best. And anyway, he made sure that you were still here to look after me and boss me around!"

When I had arrived in Mizpah after my slow walk from Ramah, I had gone immediately to Gedaliah and been surprised to find my mother there talking to him, encouraging him to search for me!

I had spoken briefly to Gedaliah, but my mother had been watching me closely and had decided that I must be either unwell or injured. She had interrupted our discussion as politely as she could and told Gedaliah that I needed looking after, as I was obviously injured. I would, she said, go home with her so that she could nurse me back to health. Gedaliah looked surprised, as if he had not noticed anything unusual about me, but offered to send a young woman to help. My mother refused his offer, saying that she could do all that I would need, then led me away to the rooms that we had been allocated.

I was glad to follow her and collapsed exhausted on a bed as soon as we arrived. The injuries that I had received from the Chaldean soldiers on the way to Ramah had made walking painful, and the extra punishment that my countrymen had inflicted on me in the compound at Ramah had left me with many extra bruises and a few open wounds that made even breathing painful.

She washed and bandaged my wounds and soothed my bruises with ointment, and soon afterwards I was left to sleep.

It was a blissful relaxation, and exhaustion and relief allowed my sleep to be the haven of rest that it had not been for some time.

I woke in the early dusk to find my mother sitting near my bed in the darkening room. She was an old, old woman, far beyond the age at which she might be expected to be caring for others, yet there she was, alert and keeping watch over me.

What an amazing woman to have as a mother!

We ate dinner together and she was all concern and compassion. After a while, though, we began to talk about the sack of Jerusalem, and then neither of us could maintain our composure. Relatives, friends, neighbours and acquaintances – we each knew of so many deaths that neither of us could describe our horror in words. After we had shared just one or two names, the tears could no longer be denied, and we wept together for the tragedy of Judah.

Neither of us wanted to start the list, but we couldn't seem to resist the urge to do so. We each shared our list of the dead that we knew about. My mother was able to tell me that my nephew Seraiah, the High Priest, had been taken away by Nebuzaradan, along with his son Jehozadak, but of our other relatives there were very few left alive. My mother had heard that my cousin Hanamel had been killed in the temple. It would only be through Seraiah that my father's line would continue. Seraiah's wife had been killed in the slaughter, and we both knew that Gemariah and Abigail had also died – and so the list went on and on.

We continued the gruesome task of itemising the dead for what seemed like hours, the tears still running down our cheeks but with no strength left for the emotion to show itself in our voices or on our faces. Maybe the fact that we had known that it was coming made it worse for us. Our family had never believed that overflowing judgement would come upon Judah, yet my mother and I had spent years anticipating the widespread punishment that God had warned of, wondering whether those we spoke to would die in the coming carnage.

So many wasted lives. Tears could not bring them back, yet we could not stop the tears.

So many years full of God's warnings ignored.

I also mentioned some who had survived, and was pleased to hear from my mother of others of whom I had not known. All of these had been taken to Ramah and must be somewhere inside that terrible compound preparing to make the long and painful journey to Babylon. I cringed as I thought of the place and its appalling conditions. How many would survive even to begin the journey? And of those, how many would survive the journey itself? – if their treatment was to be anything like that which I had experienced on my journey to Ramah.

We fell silent for a time. I did not want to report the conditions in the compound at Ramah: the screams and cries in the night; the women whose eyes were only dry because they had no more tears left to weep; the men who had attacked me in anger, yet had tears in their eyes as they did so.

I have tried before to explain how my memory of Yahweh's messages works, because it is quite different from my recall of all the other items that fill my memory. I can never forget his words, and I can read any of them in my mind whenever I choose. However, becoming consciously aware of any particular phrase can be elusive unless I keep it in my thoughts often. Otherwise, it is as if

I have lost a sign post to guide me to them. They are no longer identified with associations in my memory, nor do they spring to mind when people mention related ideas or events. My reason for mentioning this is that I suddenly and surprisingly recalled a message that had referred to Ramah, but which I had not thought of for some time. It had been part of a prophecy that had spoken of the return of the exiles:

> "Thus says the Lord:
> 'A voice is heard in Ramah,
> lamentation and bitter weeping.
> Rachel is weeping for her children;
> she refuses to be comforted for her children,
> because they are no more.' "[66]

Those words described in graphic detail exactly what I had heard in the compound at Ramah – the mothers of my people weeping and refusing to be comforted. Yet God had continued, telling us that not all the nation's children had died. There were survivors, exiles, outcasts – a remnant who would return:

> "Thus says the Lord:
> 'Keep your voice from weeping,
> and your eyes from tears,
> for there is a reward for your work, declares the Lord,
> and they shall come back from the land of the enemy.
> There is hope for your future, declares the Lord,
> and your children shall come back
> to their own country.' "[67]

All was not hopeless for Judah. God had not abandoned his people in a foreign land. The remnant would return.

---

[66] Jeremiah 31:15
[67] Jeremiah 31:16-17

Chapter 13

Gedaliah

"Your nephew Seraiah was taken to Riblah along with Zephaniah and some of the officials from the temple, I believe," said Gedaliah.

"Yes, and his sons too," I answered.

"So basically all of the chief men of Judah have been taken there: the king, his advisors and his sons, and the High Priest, his assistant and his sons."

"Do you know what has happened to them all?" I asked, particularly concerned about my nephew and his sons.

"We haven't heard yet, apart from those advisors of Zedekiah's who were killed – but you know about them already. Really, I wouldn't be surprised if Nebuchadnezzar kills all the rest of them as well."

"Except Zedekiah," I said, absently.

"He'd be the most likely one to die, I would think, given that he broke his oath to Nebuchadnezzar."

"Logically, I agree, but God said that he would be taken away into captivity rather than being killed by Nebuchadnezzar."

"Well, no doubt we'll hear all the details sometime."

"I think we can be confident that we won't see any of them again, anyway."

It was the day after my arrival in Mizpah and Gedaliah and I were sitting together in his office. I was eager to hear if there was any good news, but a little worried that he might only have more bad news to tell. I felt that I had already had more than enough of that.

"What did you see at Ramah?" asked Gedaliah.

"A collection of hopeless men, women and children being systematically abused by the Chaldeans. But it was what I heard once the sun went down that was the worst of it. Everyone is carrying their own suffering with them as pictures in their minds. Once darkness falls and their eyes can't see any more, the eyes of the mind take over. I was pre-occupied with other things, but even so, when I looked at those around me in the morning I couldn't miss the haunted look in their eyes. Terror has left its mark on everyone."

"How many people were there?"

"Somewhere between three and five thousand people in the compound I was in. Most were just sitting around aimlessly waiting to be taken away to Babylon."

"When I hear the statistics of the numbers of people being taken into captivity and those being left behind, it leaves a huge number of people unaccounted for."

"True."

"I expect that some people will have run away to stay in the surrounding countries. If they have survived, they will probably return once they hear that the Chaldeans have left – but it could take a year or two. Even allowing for many such refugees, the missing people must number in the hundreds of thousands, maybe even more."

I agreed. I had made similar calculations myself, but had found the answers too disturbing to discuss with anyone. "How much did you see on the day the Chaldeans broke in?" I asked.

"Too much. Much too much."

"Where were you?"

"In our family home. You know where it is, I mean where it *was*: not far from the temple."

"Yes, and near where the temple *was*. How did you come in contact with the Chaldeans that day?"

"I knew that they were likely to breach the wall soon – really, it was a wonder that it lasted as long as it did. Anyway, I made sure that my servants were all in the house. I was glad that I had no other close family to worry about. We started to hear shouting outside in Aramaic, but it didn't sound too threatening, so we stayed quietly inside and waited. The servants were terrified and had armed themselves with various weapons that would have been completely useless."

"So there was indeed terror on every side, just as Yahweh had warned."

"I suppose so, but when I saw their weapons, I managed to convince them to get rid of them. Having a weapon – of any sort – just gives the soldiers an excuse to kill you."

"What happened then?"

"Some soldiers banged on the door and told us all to go out into the street. Some of them went in and searched the house very quickly, then came out again and told us to go back inside and stay there."

"Were you happy to do that?"

"I must admit it did occur to me that they might seal the doors and set fire to the place, but fortunately that possibility didn't seem to occur to the servants. They were terrified enough as it was. We all went in and the soldiers left, and that's where we spent the rest of the day. Of course, we had no food and very little water, so it wasn't easy."

"I thought you were saying that you had seen some of the massacre that day."

"Yes, I did. You know that our house has... *had* two stories? Well, I spent much of the day watching out of an upstairs window. There were soldiers at the end of the street, just standing there, watching and waiting." Gedaliah stopped for a moment, staring into the distance, remembering. He turned back to me and continued, "There was a lot of smoke swirling around and it wasn't easy to see to the end of the street, but every so often I saw a Judean running past, maybe trying to escape. The Chaldean soldiers killed them all as they ran. I watched the pile of bodies building up. Every so often, the Chaldeans would grab a few of the bodies by their feet and drag them to the side so that they didn't block the street. And the pile by the side of the road kept growing throughout the day." He looked away again. "I see them every night in my dreams. I still see the bodies being dragged across the road, their heads bouncing on the cobblestones," he groaned, burying his head in his hands. "I see the corpses flung onto the pile...." His voice shook and he stopped.

We sat again in silence for a few moments.

"I was at the Potsherd Gate," I said, unable to keep silent, "when the people were caught between the Chaldeans inside the city and those outside the city. Some of those soldiers were *enjoying* it. I could see the smiles on their faces as they thrust their swords into defenceless children. I see them again too. Jerusalem is drinking the wine of God's anger. But Babylon's time will come."

"At one time, I saw half-a-dozen Judean men sneak out of a house, all armed with makeshift weapons: knives and sticks, mainly," Gedaliah continued. "They tried to make their way to the end of the street without being seen, but I had a suspicion that the soldiers had seen them as they first came out. When there was some shouting from somewhere else and the Chaldean soldiers were looking towards the noise, the men tried to attack them. But it was hopeless." Gedaliah was clenching and unclenching his fists as he spoke, and when he stopped he slowly shook his head from side to side, his face working. "The soldiers just turned around and killed them all as if they were squashing so many annoying mosquitoes. Then they came along the street, barricaded the door that the men had come out of, and set fire to the house. There were women and children in there. I heard their screams. Still, maybe that was better than the way they treated some of the women who ran past the end of the street, trying to escape...."

Gedaliah stopped. We both stopped, at a loss to know what to say or how to feel. Both of us knew that I had been predicting these things for many years and I think Gedaliah was beginning to accept that it truly had been God's will, but the horror of it all was still beyond our comprehension.

We sat in silence for a while, not looking anywhere in particular, each seeing again in our mind's eye the atrocities we had witnessed.

The door was open and, as we sat in silence, a servant walked in.

"Excuse me, my lord," he said. "Some visitors have come to see you. Their names are Ishmael, Johanan, Seraiah, … and some others I can't remember."

Gedaliah shook his head a little as if to dispel the visions and then said, "I think I might know them. Send them in."

"Should I go?" I asked.

"No, you can stay. It's probably worthwhile for you to meet these men."

The servant led six or seven men into the room as we sat waiting. It was very different from the past when entering for an audience with the king of Judah. Gedaliah may have been appointed governor, but his visitors were being welcomed into the medium-sized room in which he did much of the administrative work for which he was responsible. Nebuchadnezzar had chosen carefully when looking for a man to lead the province of Judah. Gedaliah was a natural leader and an amazingly competent administrator, but he was not in any way proud or arrogant. Some of these visitors more than made up for his lack.

The first two men seemed to be engaged in a silent struggle over who was more important and should be noticed first. One walked with a regal bearing, his head raised and a confident smile on his lips, and I recognised him instantly as Ishmael, the son of Nethaniah, a member of the royal family. The other leaned forward a little as he walked, an intense look on his face, his eyes seeking to dominate any who would meet his glance.

"Welcome, gentlemen," said Gedaliah, carefully avoiding acknowledging either one before the other.

"We hear that you have been appointed governor," said the one with the intense look. "We had to sneak in here to see you. The middle of the country and the areas around the roads to the north are still overrun with

Chaldean soldiers. Do they plan to kill us all? Should we still be fighting?"

"Yes, I am governor over Judah, Johanan," Gedaliah answered smoothly, returning his gaze resolutely. "Nebuchadnezzar is now our king, but I believe that he will leave us alone as long as we obey his commands and pay our taxes. The fighting is over. If we fight more, we will lose more."

"Johanan thinks that we can overcome the Chaldeans with the few of us that remain," said Ishmael.

"I and my men have been travelling through the south of Judah," said Johanan. "We have visited many towns, trying to bring back law and order. Most of the Chaldeans have already left that area, marching north. Many of the best vineyards and farms have been taken over by paupers, who claim that Nebuzaradan has given them the land. It's ludicrous, and at first we were just driving them off the land or giving them the whippings they deserved, but then we heard that you had been appointed governor, so we got together and came to see you. What's the situation? Is land really being given to these people?"

"It is true that Nebuzaradan has been allocating land to the poorest people," answered Gedaliah. "There are few others left anyway, and if the land is not cared for and tilled we will be overrun by wild animals."

"But they have even been taking royal land," said Ishmael disapprovingly, "land that the king and his family – my family – has owned for hundreds of years. Prime farming land. Glorious vineyards."

"Nebuchadnezzar has probably done that deliberately," said Gedaliah. "Babylon rules over Judah now, and there is no longer a Judean king or any royal family."

Ishmael looked at Gedaliah angrily, clearly not happy with what he heard. "How can you…?"

Johanan interrupted, "None of that matters as much as the question of whether we should keep fighting the Chaldeans or not. Can we trust them?"

"I have had quite a lot to do with the Chaldeans since the fall of Jerusalem and I believe that they can be trusted. They have killed huge numbers of us already and could keep going if they wanted to, but I think that the deluge of death is over for the time being. Even a brutal people like the Chaldeans eventually tires of killing and wants to move on to new vistas, new conquests – where they will probably start killing all over again."

"We can't be sure, though," grumbled Johanan. "Can you give us any sort of guarantee?"

"If the Chaldeans are giving away our land to people who don't deserve it, what else will they do?" asked Ishmael. "I can't imagine ever trusting them." He paused, then, sneering a little, said, "But then, I'm not getting paid by them."

Gedaliah ignored the barb and said reassuringly, "You don't need to be afraid of the Chaldeans. If we farm the land and live in the towns that still remain, it will be good for everyone."

"We've been fighting the Chaldeans for so long it's hard to just stop," said Johanan.

"Sometimes I wonder if we wouldn't do better to make alliances with the nations around," said Ishmael.

"You don't need to worry about the Chaldeans. I have been appointed governor, with authority to run the country for King Nebuchadnezzar, and I'm confident that this is the best thing to do – confident enough to swear an oath if you want."

Gedaliah looked around at the leaders and most of them nodded, so Gedaliah swore to them and their men, saying, "Do not be afraid to serve the Chaldeans. Dwell in the land and serve the king of Babylon, and it shall be well with you. As for me, I will dwell at Mizpah, to represent you before the Chaldeans who will come to us. But as for you, gather wine and summer fruits and oil, and store them in your vessels, and dwell in your cities that you have taken."[68]

"Isn't it a little late for the summer fruits?" asked another of the leaders, one I did not know.

"No, Seraiah," replied Gedaliah, answering my unspoken question as to who this man was – it must be Seraiah the son of Tanhumeth, another important leader in the army. "The seasons are a bit late this year. Maybe God is being kind to us, not wanting to punish us any more than he already has."

"Will God ever be kind to us again?" asked the only other man I recognised – Jezaniah the son of the Maacathite.

"Have you looked at the fruit trees?" replied another man.

"It looks like a bumper crop is coming," added the man standing next to him. The two of them looked so alike that they must have been brothers.

"Yes," agreed Gedaliah, "that is why we need as many people as possible to help with the harvest. Take your men to the villages you know and help. We need to store up food for the winter."

☙

"I thought that you would like to hear some of the news that I just received," said Gedaliah as I walked in. He looked almost excited. "It happened about two months ago, but the news has only just arrived from Riblah. You know how King Zedekiah and his sons were taken to

---

[68] Jeremiah 40:9-10

Riblah and presented before King Nebuchadnezzar. What did you expect to happen to him then?"

"I've already explained to you what God said," I replied, feeling somewhat puzzled. Gedaliah didn't normally require more than one explanation of things. I repeated God's words, mechanically:

> " 'Zedekiah king of Judah shall not escape
> out of the hand of the Chaldeans,
> but shall surely be given into the hand
> of the king of Babylon,
> and shall speak with him face to face
> and see him eye to eye.
> And he shall take Zedekiah to Babylon,
> and there he shall remain until I visit him,
> declares the Lord. ' "[69]

"Yes," said Gedaliah, "I remember alright, and that's why I'm telling you this. Zedekiah is to be taken to Babylon as a prisoner – it happened *exactly* as you said it would – but there was another amazing twist to it as well. Nebuchadnezzar was talking to Zedekiah – you know, 'face to face' and 'eye to eye', as you said – but then he took Zedekiah's sons and killed them before him."

"Poor Zedekiah!" I replied.

"True, but I expected that anyway. This is the amazing part, though: Nebuchadnezzar gave the order and his men gouged out Zedekiah's eyes[70] with a bar of bronze taken out of a fire. So the last thing he will *ever* see with his eyes is Nebuchadnezzar."

"The one to whom he had given his word, which he then broke."

"Yes. It all fits in with what you said – but I'm fairly sure that you didn't imagine it would happen in quite that

---

[69] Jeremiah 32:4-5
[70] Jeremiah 39:6-7; 52:10-11

way! There is also a special message for you from Nebuzaradan. He says that when Zedekiah was told what was to happen to him, he said that you had predicted most of the details already.[71]

I was astonished and excited by Gedaliah's recounting of the events. True, God's message had said nothing about Zedekiah's eyes being gouged out, but it had mentioned him speaking to Nebuchadnezzar face to face and seeing him eye to eye, and now he would never be able to do that again.[72]

It seemed fitting, somehow.

"Nebuzaradan's message finished with the words, 'You were right again.' "

"It wasn't me," I said; "it was God. How could I have predicted that?"

"Well, it's amazing, that's what I say," replied Gedaliah, and paused, his face alight. After a few moments, however, his face became sombre and he continued, "But there is also some more sad news for you from Riblah. Your nephew, Seraiah, was killed, along with Zephaniah, the second priest. However, your great-nephew Jehozadak is alright – he is being taken to Babylon as a captive, so the line of high priests will continue. There were quite a few others killed there as well, including seven of the king's councillors. Then all of the survivors were taken away to Babylon. Even now they will be walking to Babylon without any realistic hope of return. You did say seventy years, didn't you?"[73]

"Yes," I said wearily, feeling completely mixed up: elated, but sad. We had all seen and heard of so much

---

[71] Jeremiah 32:4-5; 34:3-5; 38:23

[72] The prophet Ezekiel was also told that Zedekiah would go to the land of Babylon but *would not see it* (Ezekiel 12:13).

[73] Jeremiah 25:11-12; 29:10

death over the last few months that we could dismiss the death of my nephew and Zephaniah casually in just a few words – and then move on.

"All the bronze from the temple and any other treasures they found have also been taken. There's nothing much left of Jerusalem now but piles of stones – and burnt ones at that."

"God told me on several occasions that the city would burn, yet even as the end approached, he still offered Zedekiah one last chance to avoid it by surrendering. But he wouldn't listen."

As I was speaking, Gedaliah's servant entered the room and once I finished, he reported that the commanders of the resistance forces had come to see Gedaliah again.

"Should I leave this time?" I asked.

"I don't think you need to."

I sat and waited as the men were brought in again. This time, Ishmael the son of Nethaniah was not with them.

Johanan was their spokesman, and began abruptly, "We have important, secret news for you." His eyes drifted towards me questioningly as he spoke.

Gedaliah waved his hand towards me, saying, "You must all know of Jeremiah, the prophet. Is it alright for him to hear the news?"

Johanan looked at me doubtfully, but all of the others were nodding their assent and eventually he too nodded in agreement before continuing, "Do you know that Baalis the king of the Ammonites has sent Ishmael the son of Nethaniah to take your life?"[74]

"Oh, I can't believe that," said Gedaliah with a laugh.

---

[74] Jeremiah 40:13-14

"It's true. We have heard it from one of our informers, and also directly from one of his men."

"You must all know that it's not hard to get people to give bad reports about leaders. I'm sure you could get some bad reports about me if you went looking for them. Ishmael may not be your best friend, but there is no reason to believe that he's a traitor."

"What reason could he have for visiting Baalis?"

"No doubt he was warning him about the Chaldeans. Remember, he is a member of the old royal family, so he probably knows many of the kings around."

The leaders tried individually to convince Gedaliah of the seriousness of the situation, but he would not believe them.

If only he had listened.

After a while, they gave up and the subject turned to the amazing harvest that the people had been collecting all over the land. They marvelled at the abundance that would be available for the coming winter – and what a contrast it was to the previous winter when we had all endured such famine and disease. Yet much of the magnificent harvest would have fallen to the ground and rotted had it not been for the help of large numbers of Judeans who had returned from the surrounding nations where they had fled to escape from king Nebuchadnezzar.

☙

I didn't hear of it until after the disaster had played itself out, but apparently later that day, Johanan returned, alone, to see Gedaliah. He offered to kill Ishmael and thwart his plans – his undercover work for Baalis.

But Gedaliah refused to allow it.

Chapter 14

Confusion

October, 587 BC – the seventh month

"I have lived a long life, Jeremiah. So much has happened since your father died more than 30 years ago." My mother's voice quavered and she sounded old, though her thoughts were still clear and precise.

The late summer harvest had finished and mountains of delicious fruit had helped to strengthen the few survivors who remained in the land – the poor who were now rich. Everyone was busy, and sometimes the hard physical work of each day was an antidote to the nightmares that made the hours of darkness times of terror for so many. But no-one had been left untouched by the indiscriminate slaughter that had surrounded the fall of Jerusalem, and many were now turning to new wine for comfort.

"Yes," I agreed. "Josiah was king, then, and there was still hope. I thought that maybe all of this could be avoided."

We were sitting on a wooden seat in the golden light of the afternoon sun outside our house in Mizpah. The weather was balmy, and a few puffy white clouds drifted slowly across the sky on a gentle breeze. Peace and tranquility enveloped the scene, as if all the problems of the world were nothing but scattered memories, as harmless as the clouds that floated above. But thirty tragic years of history could not be ignored.

"We could not turn around and walk with God, my son. Our nation was too steeped in generations of unfaithfulness to learn faithfulness without force and horror. God tried. You tried. We all tried. But in the end it was only this tragedy that could turn us back to Yahweh – and even that disaster hasn't turned us back yet. Seventy full years of suffering may be what it takes. I won't live to see it, but I pray for it every day." My mother looked tired and leaned back against the warm stones of the house, closing her eyes.

"I won't see it either," I replied, "but God's occasional pictures of our regathering fill me with hope for the future."

There was silence for a few moments, and I wondered if she had gone to sleep. But then she opened her eyes and said, "I'm tired and can't think very well. Remind me of what he has shown you."

Once more, she closed her eyes, waiting for me to paint the pictures of hope that I had heard in the words of Yahweh. I took a deep breath and tried to organise my thoughts. Over the past six weeks in Mizpah, I had spent considerable time making the most of my reconciliation with God, familiarising myself once again with his messages to me. However, there were so many that it was not an easy task. I had tried to categorise them by audience, to arrange them in order or to group them by theme, but no single method seemed to work very well. In some cases, God had given me messages more than ten years apart that were almost identical, and a simple chronological ordering didn't do them justice. Scrolls of most of the words, written in my own untidy scrawl, had survived in the care of my mother, and these made the task easier.

As God had promised, Baruch the son of Neriah had survived the destruction of Jerusalem, and over the last month we had discussed the scrolls that he had made of God's words to me. Many new messages had been added over the years since he had begun the task, and the messages had ended up spread across several scrolls and letters. Baruch and I believed that many of these must have been destroyed in the conflagration. Both ancient libraries and modern collections of business documents had been consumed when the Chaldeans had set fire to all of the major buildings. I couldn't help wondering what had happened to the title deed for the land in Anathoth that I had bought from my cousin Hanamel as a parable. Baruch and I had been working on organising and again writing out all of God's words to me and some of the surrounding events where they were important, but it was hard to decide on the best order.

"Jeremiah, have you gone to sleep?" asked my mother.

"No," I said, smiling, "I'm just trying to get organised."

"But don't you still remember all of the words God has spoken to you?"

"Yes, but if you don't want to listen to them all in order from beginning to end, I need to work out which ones to tell you! You only wanted the ones about a future hope, so let's start with one about the 70 years that you mentioned."

"I love that one."

I read it from the wall of my mind, words of beauty and grace:

<blockquote>
" 'For thus says the Lord:
When seventy years are completed for Babylon,
I will visit you, and I will fulfil to you my promise
and bring you back to this place.
For I know the plans I have for you,
declares the Lord,
plans for welfare and not for evil,
to give you a future and a hope.
Then you will call upon me
and come and pray to me,
and I will hear you.
You will seek me and find me,
when you seek me with all your heart.
I will be found by you, declares the Lord,
and I will restore your fortunes
and gather you from all the nations
and all the places where I have driven you,
declares the Lord,
and I will bring you back to the place
from which I sent you into exile.' "[75]
</blockquote>

"Will any of my great-grandsons – Seraiah's sons – return here to be priests? Or maybe his grandsons or great-grandsons?"

"I'm sure they will, mother.[76] Maybe Jehozadak,[77] or

---

[75] Jeremiah 29:10-14

[76] Jeremiah 33:18

[77] It appears that Jehozadak had died before the nation returned, but that his son Joshua (or Jeshua) returned as High Priest. See 1 Chronicles 6:14-15; Ezra 2:1-2; Haggai 1:1; Zechariah 6:11.

even little Ezra.[78] What about this one, mother? It talks about offspring as you are, and God gave me this message twice – it was exactly the same each time:

" 'Then fear not, O Jacob my servant, declares the Lord,
nor be dismayed, O Israel;
for behold, I will save you from far away,
and your offspring from the land of their captivity.
Jacob shall return and have quiet and ease,
and none shall make him afraid.' "[79]

"What a change that will be: 'none shall make him afraid'," she replied. "It seems that there have always been nations to make us afraid, ever since Josiah went to fight Pharaoh Neco."

"Do you remember that yoke I had to wear[80] – the one that Hananiah broke?[81] I suppose it was seven years ago now that he broke it."

"Yes. It was hard to watch when so many people laughed at you."

"Well, just before that message I just quoted, there was an occasion when God talked about breaking the yoke from our neck, and then he said:

" 'Behold, I will restore the fortunes of the tents of Jacob
and have compassion on his dwellings;
the city shall be rebuilt on its mound,
and the palace shall stand where it used to be.' "[82]

"Help me to get that straight. Does it mean that no-one will rebuild Jerusalem until Babylon doesn't rule over us anymore?" she asked.

---

[78] Ezra 7:1-6

[79] Jeremiah 30:10; 46:27

[80] See Volume 3 – Darkness Falling, Chapter 11

[81] See Volume 4 – The Darkness Deepens, Chapter 12

[82] Jeremiah 30:18

"I suppose so. In the time of King Hezekiah, Micah said:

> " 'Zion shall be ploughed as a field;
> Jerusalem shall become a heap of ruins,
> and the mountain of the house a wooded height.'[83]

"Even with no-one living there, it will take a long time for a place like the temple to become a 'wooded height'," I said.

"So Jerusalem will be left in ruins until Babylon is defeated?"

"Yes."

"And then our people will come back and set up a kingdom again?"

I frowned. It was a question that I had spent a lot of time thinking about. More than once, God had spoken about a branch from David ruling over Judah and Israel after the return from captivity – presumably a descendant of David. But God had also spoken of a prince whom he would call to approach him. It sounded a little different from just continuing the dynasty. And which dynasty anyway? Zedekiah's sons were all dead, and God had dismissed Jeconiah with the words:

> "Write this man down as childless,
> a man who shall not succeed in his days,
> for none of his offspring shall succeed
> in sitting on the throne of David
> and ruling again in Judah."[84]

"I'm not sure," I said, finally. "We *will* have a king whom God invites to be king, but it may not be a descendant of Jeconiah or Zedekiah. I'm not sure. But it must be a descendant of David."

---

[83] Micah 3:12
[84] Jeremiah 22:30

"Of course," agreed mother. We had often talked about God's promise that David would have a descendant who would rule forever.[85]

"There is another prophecy that shines out like the sun for me," I said. "Or two suns really, because it is another of the prophecies that God has given twice in almost exactly the same words. He gave it to two different prophets: Micah and Isaiah. In Micah's prophecy, it comes immediately after the part where God talks about the temple site being like a forest. It says:

" 'It shall come to pass in the latter days
that the mountain of the house of the Lord
shall be established as the highest of the mountains,
and it shall be lifted up above the hills;
and peoples shall flow to it,
and many nations shall come, and say:
"Come, let us go up to the mountain of the Lord,
to the house of the God of Jacob,
that he may teach us his ways
and that we may walk in his paths."
For out of Zion shall go forth the law,
and the word of the Lord from Jerusalem.
He shall judge between many peoples,
and shall decide for strong nations far away;
and they shall beat their swords into ploughshares,
and their spears into pruning hooks;
nation shall not lift up sword against nation,
neither shall they learn war anymore.' "[86]

She sighed and said, "It is beautiful. A lovely thought to remember as I come to the end of my life."

---

[85] 1 Chronicles 17:11-12

[86] Micah 4:1-3 (see Isaiah 2:2-4 for the same message with just a few words in four lines that are different in a way that is symmetrical).

"It really is something special, isn't it?" I didn't like my mother's mention of the end of her life. I still felt that I needed her support.

"You know," she continued, "that sounds like a time of greater power for Israel than even Solomon ever had."

"True."

"And you say that the same prophecy was given to Isaiah too? That must mean it is very sure. Yahweh must also want us to notice it."

"Yes. I read it first in my 'smelly scroll' of Isaiah, and only came across it in Micah some time later. I have been reading Isaiah again recently. I'm so thankful that you were able to bring it with you from Jerusalem – it really is my most precious possession. Did you know that Isaiah was also told about Israel returning from Babylon[87] and about a branch from God?"[88]

"No. I would like to hear more about that later, but first, what about us and people like us? Will we ever see the temple rebuilt? For those of us who have seen so much horror – what will there be for us? We will not see the nation return."

"Abraham was promised the land of Israel and never received it, but God always keeps his promises, so Abraham must live again. There are some delightful thoughts about living again in Isaiah too. One particular passage always gives me goosebumps. I'll go and get the scroll and find the place, so that I can make sure I don't make any mistakes."

"Alright. If this magnificent sunshine has put me to sleep by the time you return, please wake me up."

I stood, went into the house and found my scroll of Isaiah's prophecies. As I walked outside again, I also

---

[87] Isaiah 48:20

[88] Isaiah 4:2; 11:1

carried a small table with me, to rest the scroll on. My mother had indeed gone to sleep and her face looked peaceful and relaxed as she leaned against the wall, bathed in the late afternoon sun. I sat down and unrolled my precious scroll until I found the place I wanted, the familiar, slightly musty smell tickling my nostrils. For the first time I realised that I no longer found the smell unpleasant.

There was no need to wake my mother immediately, so I sat in the sunshine and considered all the help my mother had given me over the years. How much harder would my life have been without her?

I had no doubt that she was a true daughter of her parents, a couple who had been too outspoken about Yahweh to remain in Jerusalem during the reign of Manasseh. Her love of the word of Yahweh was the inspiration for my own devotion to him – although she would probably argue that my father had had a hand in it too. Maybe that had been true when I was too young to remember anything, but my memories recalled only conflict between us.

After a few minutes, I reached across and put my hand on her arm, and she woke immediately – instantly alert in a way that was quite astonishing for one of her age.

"Thank you for waking me. I love to hear you reading God's word, and particularly anything about a hope for the future. Read it, please."

I began to read:

" 'Your dead shall live; their bodies shall rise.
You who dwell in the dust, awake and sing for joy!
For your dew is a dew of light,
and the earth will give birth to the dead.' "[89]

---

[89] Isaiah 26:19

"We haven't had much singing for joy recently. When will it be?"

"I don't know," I admitted. "I have had to learn to wait patiently for Yahweh's prophecies to be fulfilled. But when they do finally begin to be fulfilled, they often seem to come in a rush."

"I hope so."

∞

It was the last time I ever spoke to my mother.

Our conversation had been happy, and the memory of it has helped me through the black and lonely times that have followed.

We had shared our love for God and had joyfully discussed his plans for Israel – and for Babylon. As the cool of evening settled in, we went inside and I left to do more work with Baruch on the scrolls he was completing for me.

By the time I returned, she had already gone to bed.

In the morning, I arose before dawn as usual and went out to pray. When I returned, I took her a drink, as I often did when we were living in the same house.

I found her sleeping peacefully, but could not wake her.

That day I faced a terrible conflict. God had forbidden me to join in mourning for the dead, and I had obeyed his command following the deaths of my father and my two brothers. Must I also do the same for my mother? God had stated that the reason was because he had taken away his peace from the land and multitudes would die with no-one to mourn them. Surely that time had ended with the destruction of Jerusalem? Could I not now mourn the death of my mother and arrange her burial? Yet God had not released me from that constraint, so I concluded with a heavy heart that I must still obey – not mourning even for my mother. Sadly, later events showed that God's anger with Judah was not exhausted because our disobedience was not yet complete. Many more were still to die as a result.

My mother had outlived her parents, her siblings, her husband, two of her sons and even some of her grandsons. I was her only close family left, and about as popular as a leper. Nevertheless, she saw God and those who walked with God as her family, and she died in faith that God would fulfil his promises.

Since I could not arrange the funeral, Gedaliah arranged the burial of my mother in Mizpah as a friend of the family. Nebuchadnezzar had made strict laws about Jerusalem and what could be done within its ruins. Burials were forbidden, so my mother could not be buried with her husband.

You may wonder, as I did, what would have happened if Gedaliah had not been there? How would my mother have been buried if I could not do it? But God really does provide when we obey. Always – and often in the most unobtrusive of ways.

Gedaliah and I spoke after the burial was complete and I told him how grateful I was for his help. I'm glad that I was able to do so.

⊂⊃

Two days later, I was sitting in the afternoon sun once more when a Judean soldier came around the corner of the house. He held a sword and had a determined look on his face.

"Come with me," he said.

"Why?" I asked.

He took a step towards me, lifting his sword threateningly. "Don't ask questions," he said, "just come. Now!"

I followed him and he led me to the small central square of Mizpah. About fifty frightened people stood around in small groups, guarded by three soldiers. Ishmael the son of Nethaniah stood at one end of the square and was clearly in charge. I was pushed hurriedly into the square and then the soldier left again, presumably to look for more people.

As we stood there, everyone except the soldiers looked confused. This was one surprise too many, and everyone seemed to have lost their ability to process events. We waited passively, obeying any instructions we were given by the soldiers without thought or question. We had all exhausted our need to understand.

From time to time, soldiers ushered others into the square in ones and twos, and after a while I pulled myself together to look around me. A group of terrified young girls stood not far from Ishmael, and I presumed that they must be the king's daughters, who had been entrusted to Gedaliah. But where was Gedaliah? Others I recognised from having seen them around the town – some of the poorest people in the land who had been given land around Mizpah, but who still lived in fear and preferred to stay within the walls of the town. Another distinctive group of men stood huddled together near Ishmael, and I was sure that I did not recognise any of them. They looked very peculiar: their beards shaved off and their clothes torn. Through the holes in their clothes, I could see recent gashes on their bodies that were just starting to heal.

After a while I decided to go across to them and find out who they were – if the guards would let me do so. I began to edge my way slowly towards them without making any movements that might have appeared purposeful. No-one stopped me, and eventually I was standing next to one of the men.

"Who are you?" I asked quietly.

He looked at me in fright, and then his eyes flitted to Ishmael, who was busy giving instructions to one of his men. Encouraged by the fact that no-one seemed to be noticing us, he answered even more softly, "We were eighty men from Shechem, Shiloh and Samaria who were bringing grain offerings and incense to present at the temple of the Lord."

More people were still being brought into the square, and in the hubbub we were left in peace for a time.

"Didn't you know that the temple has been destroyed?" I asked.

"We had been told it, but we wanted to make some offerings there anyway – as part of atoning for our guilt as a nation."

"Where are the rest of your companions?"

"Ishmael and his men killed them all!"

"What, seventy men? Killed?"

"Yes. Ishmael came out of the town to meet us this morning. He was weeping and looking very upset. He said to us, 'Come in to Gedaliah the son of Ahikam.' We assumed that some terrible accident must have happened, and we trusted him. There were ten men with him, and as we came into the city, they started to kill us all. We had no weapons and nowhere to run. I was near the back of the group, and I begged them not to put me to death. I told them that I had hidden stores of wheat, barley, oil, and honey. It took some fast talking, but eventually I managed to convince them. The rest of my friends here confirmed my story, and added that they had hidden stores as well. So we lived."

The story had been told in a hurried undertone. It seemed unbelievable, but how could I be sure? "What did they do with the bodies?"

"They threw them into a huge cistern, and forced us to help them too."

The story seemed to fit together. There was a large cistern in Mizpah, one that King Asa had made as part of the defences against Baasha the king of Israel hundreds of years before.

"But what about Gedaliah? Did he know anything about this?"

"Ishmael said that Gedaliah was a traitor, and that…"

Some more people were being herded into the square at that moment and there was little room left to put them. One of Ishmael's soldiers approached the group with which I was standing.

"You men from the north," he shouted, "come over here and stand by yourselves. We don't want you getting mixed up with the rest of them."

I stepped away unobtrusively as they were led to a corner of the square and the soldier moved to stand between them and the rest of us in the square.

Was the story true? And what had the man been about to say? What had happened to Gedaliah?

Chapter 15

Escape from Ishmael

Ishmael's men continued to round up the people of Mizpah, and as I waited in the square, I remembered that the field commanders had warned Gedaliah that Ishmael was working for Baalis, the king of the Ammonites. They had said that he had been sent to kill Gedaliah. At the time, it had seemed ridiculous – why would Baalis pick a fight with the Chaldeans by killing the governor they had appointed? – but now it seemed the only explanation that made any sense.

As I wondered what to do, I was surprised by a voice from behind.

"I see they got you too, Jeremiah."

I turned and saw that it was Baruch. "Yes," I said. By that time the square was quite crowded, but I didn't want to be overheard. "Do you know where Gedaliah is?" I asked urgently, but as quietly as I could. "Do you have any news?"

"Isn't Gedaliah here? I thought he must be the one organising all of this and wondered what was going on."

"I'm worried about him," I said. "Ishmael over there – do you know him?"

Baruch nodded, and the look on his face wasn't complimentary to Ishmael. "I wouldn't trust him as far as I could throw him," he said. "I did some work for him once."

"Well, he and his men seem to have murdered at least seventy men so far today, and probably Gedaliah as well." As quickly as possible, I explained the news that I had heard from the pilgrims. Just as I finished, I saw Ishmael looking at us. "Stop looking so shocked," I hissed urgently, "or we might be the next to go. Ishmael has spotted us and is coming this way with one of his men." A thrill of fear went through me.

Ishmael made his way through the crowd right up to us, the soldier close at his heels, sword in hand.

"Baruch," said Ishmael brusquely, ignoring me completely, "we need a scribe. We have to send a message to Johanan and his friends."

"You mean Johanan, the son of Kareah?"

"Yes, Mister High-and-Mighty Johanan."

"Do you have any paper? Your soldier wouldn't let me bring any with me, or any ink or pens. I don't think he liked the look of my scribe's knife."

"There should be some in the administration offices. They're not far away. Go with Ram" – he gestured to the soldier who stood behind him – "and find whatever you need to write the message. Ram knows what the message is and will tell you what to write."

Baruch agreed and left with Ram, while Ishmael returned to his place, supervising his men. Ram and Baruch were gone for quite a while, and as time passed, Ishmael grew more and more on edge. When he sent out the soldiers to continue the search for others in the city, he urged them to hurry. Time, he said, was short, and we must all leave soon. I wondered what that meant.

Baruch was still absent when another voice came from behind. This time the speaker was Ebed-melech, the Ethiopian who had saved my life so courageously when I had been thrown into a cistern deep in the palace.

"Excuse me, sir, I'm sorry to see that you have been caught again. I had hoped that God might have taken you away as he did with Elijah."

"God doesn't do those sorts of things in modern times – and anyway, he only did it with his great prophets, not people like me. I'm glad to see you, Ebed-melech, but sorry to see you here. I thought that you would be out at your farm, beyond the reach of this latest disaster."

"I came in to bring some food for the governor – so much food has grown in just the last month, it's amazing. I've never done any farming before, and I thought it must be hard based on the complaining I've heard so often from farmers. But this has been easy!"

"I wish you had stayed on the farm today."

"Yahweh must have wanted me here. Let's wait and see what happens."

As we spoke, Baruch at last returned, accompanied by Ram. They skirted the crowd, making their way towards Ishmael.

"Follow me," I said to Ebed-melech, and began to force my way through the crowd to where Ishmael stood. I didn't want to get too close, but I did want to hear what was said.

"Here is the message, my lord," said Ram, holding up a sealed scroll. "It's all ready to be sent."

"Give it here," said Ishmael. "I'll just read it quickly."

"Well, sir," said Ram, doubtfully, "you can if you want to, but it's all sealed up – I used your seal."

"That's alright," he said taking the scroll. "We can seal it up again before you leave."

"We don't have any more clay here for sealing," said Baruch, seeming ill at ease.

"Well, I guess it doesn't really need sealing at all," said Ishmael, turning the scroll around to locate the seal. "Ram will be the one carrying the message anyway."

"I doubt that Johanan will believe that a message like that is from you if it isn't sealed," said Baruch. "Would you trust an unsealed scroll with a message like that?"

"Hmm, maybe not," said Ishmael. "But we can still seal it again later."

"Excuse me sir," said Ram, "but don't you want to leave as soon as possible? We don't want to get surprised here – we'd be badly outnumbered if Johanan turned up where he wasn't wanted."

"Yes, you're right," said Ishmael, looking around as if he expected to see Johanan stride arrogantly into the square at any moment. "Anyway, did you and Baruch discuss the message at all?"

"Yes," replied Ram, "Baruch suggested some minor changes and I agreed to them. It is very nicely worded, sir. Convincing."

Ishmael looked satisfied and gave the scroll back to Ram, who tucked it away in the bag he had slung across his shoulders. The two hurried away and I made my way to Baruch, with Ebed-melech behind me. "What were you looking worried about?" I asked.

Baruch greeted Ebed-melech warmly, and then said softly, "I was terrified that he was going to open that scroll. You see, while I was writing the message, Ram had to leave the room for a few minutes, so I took the opportunity to scrawl a quick note to Johanan, telling him what had really happened. After Ram had read over Ishmael's message, I suggested that it would be best to seal it up before we went back, otherwise there would be a delay while Ishmael went to get some clay to seal it. He agreed and I took the scroll and rolled it up tightly, taking care to slip my message inside it first. Then I quickly tied the string around the outside and folded the clay over it and Ram sealed it with Ishmael's seal."

"No wonder you were worried!"

"I talked with Ram as we walked there, and he hinted that Gedaliah was dead. Then, when we went into Gedaliah's office, there was dried blood everywhere. I looked at him straight and asked whether they had killed Gedaliah and all of his men. He admitted that they had, and then I made an inspired guess, asking him what had happened to the Chaldean soldiers in the city. He said that they had killed all of them too."

I think my mouth may have been hanging open as he explained all of this. I was overcome by the scale of Ishmael's crimes and wondered where this would all lead. I was glad that my mother had not been forced to suffer this extra disaster, particularly given that she had known Gedaliah since he was a baby.

"That wasn't all," Baruch continued. "Ram also mentioned that we will all be leaving Mizpah soon — hurrying to Baalis the king of the Ammonites, but taking a roundabout way through Gibeon so that Johanan and the others will never guess where we've gone. So I put that in my note as well."

"How did you get him to be so talkative?"

Baruch laughed. "Oh, I was just my normal friendly self." But then he became serious again. "How could they have been so brutal?" he asked. "So many killed, and all to help Baalis? Does that traitor Ishmael seriously think he can get away with it?"

"I think he is about as humble as Johanan."

"Probably. Those field commanders all seem to think that they are the only ones who know anything about anything."

Ebed-melech had been listening to this conversation, but looked rather lost as he tried to catch up with the terrible news.

"Are you saying that Ishmael and his men have killed Gedaliah?" he asked.

"Yes, along with of all his men, all the Chaldeans, and about 70 pilgrims who were innocently passing through," I said.

"And now he is planning to go across to the Ammonites and take us with him?"

"So it appears."

"And you, Baruch, wrote a secret note to go with Ishmael's message? What would have happened if he had found the note?"

"I suppose he would have killed me," Baruch answered simply. "But Johanan had to know the truth."

"If Ram is going to deliver this message," I asked Baruch, "what will he do when he sees Johanan open Ishmael's message and take out your note?"

Baruch looked at me with wide eyes and said, "I hadn't thought about that!"

"Well, I don't think we need to worry about it. God said that he would look after you, didn't he? He has certainly been doing so today, and I'm sure he will find a way to make it all work."

Ebed-melech nodded, but Baruch still looked worried for a few moments. Then he shrugged, smiled a little crookedly and said, "Yes, I suppose he will."

℞

"Listen to me, everyone," shouted Ishmael as his men tried to quiet the crowd. "We're sorry to cause you all such inconvenience today, but it was the only way to save your lives. You may hear a few stories flying around, but most of them are wrong. I thought it was important to tell you all the truth so that you will know what is really going on."

He had everyone's attention by then, and I was amazed to hear that he planned to tell us the truth.

"You all know that Gedaliah was appointed governor by Nebuchadnezzar," said Ishmael, "and we all trusted him to negotiate with the Chaldeans on our behalf. Unfortunately, though, Gedaliah has turned traitor. We trusted him and he has betrayed us. Just yesterday, I went to see him, and he tried to convince me to help him in his terrible plans. Me! A member of the royal family of Judah! He wanted me to stay here and keep you all calm and quiet while he went north to fetch more Chaldean soldiers. He plans to bring them back here and kill everyone in the city, on the pretext that some of you have been planning to rebel."

The surviving pilgrims were sitting in one corner of the square with two of Ishmael's soldiers nearby. One of the pilgrims began to stand – it was clear that he wanted to say something – but the soldier nearest him laid a hand threateningly on his sword hilt and the man subsided.

Baruch, Ebed-melech and I were looking at each other, but we all decided that it was best to keep silent. So this was the "truth" as Ishmael saw it – or at least the tale he wanted us to believe. Where would it lead us, I wondered?

"We are very lucky to have found this out before the Chaldeans arrived to slaughter us all," continued Ishmael. "But now we need to escape as quickly as possible, heading south. I and my men will help to lead you to safety, but time is of the essence. We need to leave right now. There is no time for any of you to gather any more belongings or anything else. No time even for questions. Follow me, and be very careful to obey any instructions that my men give you."

Ishmael turned and led the way to the gate of Mizpah, a crowd of worried people following him. As I walked through the gate I wondered what we could do. Soldiers marched both in front and behind, hurrying the rest of the crowd as we set off southward.

Ram had left some time before, travelling to the place where the other field commanders had been gathered. There was no way of knowing, but I wondered whether the trigger for Ishmael's brutal rampage had been the fact that he had not been invited to that gathering of field commanders.

We walked southward as quickly as Ishmael and his men could drive us, but it was not like a marching column of soldiers, or even a caravan of traders used to travelling together. Instead, it was a mixed group of young and old, men and women, boys and girls, and we set a slow pace that clearly upset Ishmael. When we reached the place where the road to Gibeon branched off from the main road, we followed it, Ishmael and his men relaxing visibly once we were out of sight of the main road.

Birds were already flying overhead when I awoke in the early dawn. We had stopped for the night near the great pool in Gibeon, and it had been brought home to me again just how few people were left in Judah. Gibeon had changed from the bustling, busy town that I remembered when I had been travelling around Judah and Israel delivering God's warnings, into a quiet, empty shell. There were no city guardians to challenge Ishmael or question his intentions with such a large company of people. We had settled down to camp for the night near the pool, but only a few inhabitants had walked timidly past us to fetch water. Soon after our arrival, Ram had hurried up the road, fresh from delivering the message to Johanan. Apparently he had handed over the scroll and left before it was opened. Baruch and I looked at each other and smiled when we heard this. God had indeed taken care of Baruch, just as we had been confident he would.

Ishmael and his men said nothing explicitly to suggest that we were prisoners, but they did made it clear that we shouldn't move far from where we were lying. Darkness fell, and those of us who knew more of the truth of Ishmael's behaviour took the opportunity to share some of our knowledge with others. Before we all settled down to sleep, most people knew about the deaths of Gedaliah, the Chaldean soldiers and the seventy pilgrims. As survivors of the terrible destruction of the kingdom of Judah, this was just another disaster that threatened their survival. Nobody wanted to challenge Ishmael with their new knowledge, though, and it was a subdued group of people who prepared for sleep that night.

Few were carrying any bedding, so most of us had to make do with 'the traveller's bed': cloaks wrapped closely around us with a few layers folded under the hip and a flat stone for a pillow.

Ishmael's ten men were spread around us in twos, but no unexpected events disturbed our rest, and when I opened my eyes in the morning it was still too dark to see any movement around me. The only visible activity was in the autumn sky above, where birds were travelling south to avoid the coming cold of winter. No sun was yet visible, but the slowly growing light in the east heralded its approach. The waning moon – a delicate sliver of exquisite beauty – hung just above the horizon, with a halo of light surrounding it. Once again, God had delivered a scene of transcendent loveliness just when I needed a little encouragement. It seemed ridiculous to think that this largesse had been prepared exclusively for me, but it was not hard to appreciate its beauty and praise God for it. In looking back over my life, I am amazed by the number of times when I can remember God being revealed as the master artist through the beauty of a sunrise or sunset, or even a passing alignment of common events that for an instant touches the heart with wonder. God was encouraging me again, but I still mourned the loss of one with whom I could share my appreciation of his gentle hand. My mother was dead, and there was no-one with whom I could share my thankfulness.

I was about to start praying when I heard a voice from next to me – proving me wrong. The voice was quiet, but filled with a sense of wonder. "Sir, do you see the moon just hanging there, waiting for the sun to come up and join it? How could anyone see such a heavenly sight without worshipping the king of heaven?"

It was Ebed-melech, also awake in the early dawn, and we lay side by side for a few moments, captive to the beauty that God puts on show for any who look for it. Then I broke the silence, taking the opportunity to explain how prayer, coupled with the beauty seen in sunrises and sunsets, had been a tower of strength to me through over forty years of prophesying. After that we each prayed, alone in a crowd that was being guarded by a group of ruthless killers who felt completely in control of events, without any need for Yahweh.

The noises of migrating birds continued to float down on the breezes, and gradually the encampment awoke and we concluded our urgent prayers for God's protection.

I didn't notice anything unusual until a man near us asked, "Who are they?" He was pointing towards the road by which we had arrived the previous night. A group of maybe a hundred men was hurrying along the road towards us.

"Halt!" shouted the guard who was closest to the approaching men.

They ignored him, drawing quickly closer.

"Isn't the man at the front Johanan, the son of Kareah?" asked Ebed-melech.

"I think you're right," I said, peering at the group. "And I think those two running close to each other are the sons of Ephai. They look so alike."

The news spread rapidly through the crowd that Judean soldiers were approaching, with the famous field commanders leading them.

"Johanan has come to save us," shouted someone, and many cheered.

"Let's escape from Ishmael and his men while they're too busy to stop us," yelled another, and a chorus of voices agreed.

Ishmael's men had gathered together to meet the threat of Johanan and his men, and their swords were ready in their hands. For a few moments at least, they were ignoring us, and some of the group began to run towards the approaching soldiers, skirting around Ishmael and his men. Some of the men saw the breakaway and moved to cut off their escape, but Ishmael called them back. Soon all of us had run past our erstwhile guards and were hurrying towards the oncoming rescuers, who were moving much more slowly now as they neared Ishmael's band.

"Give up, Ishmael," shouted Johanan.

"Never!" replied Ishmael. "You are all traitors, friends of the Chaldeans, cowards!"

At that, Johanan ran forward, with his men close behind. He struck at Ishmael with his sword, but the stroke was parried. The soldiers with Johanan each picked their own target, and battle was joined. Johanan had more men, but it was clear that Ishmael's men were far better trained.

However, the overwhelming force of numbers was with Johanan, and it was not long before Ishmael and his men turned and ran, leaving behind two men who lay dead on the road. More of Johanan's men had fallen, but the victory was his.

There were many greetings and explanations, and eventually everyone agreed that it would be best to return to Mizpah. Within two hours we were all back in Mizpah, and everyone, including Johanan and his men could see for themselves the piled bodies of pilgrims, Chaldean soldiers and Gedaliah's men, filling the cistern of Asa.

Everyone was terrified. All of the Chaldean soldiers that Nebuchadnezzar had left were dead. Gedaliah and his staff were dead also, and everybody could see that retribution was sure to come. Nebuchadnezzar's recent fury against Jerusalem would be as nothing compared with his response to this atrocity.

℃℞

No-one was willing to stay in Mizpah. There were too many dead bodies, and too much that promised death to the living. To stay seemed to be to invite inevitable destruction by the Chaldeans.

By the end of the afternoon of our return from Gibeon, everybody was on edge: how long would it be before an army marched over the horizon and brought our doom?

The field commanders met and decided that we must leave the very next morning. Anything that could not be left behind must be packed before dawn.

It rained heavily that night, and we left first thing in the morning.

Our destination? It was not decided yet, but somewhere south of Jerusalem – the most recent target of Nebuchadnezzar's fury.

Fear lent speed to fleeing feet, and before night fell, the company had reached Chimham's Inn at Bethlehem.

Our destination was settled too: Egypt.

We had planned to continue our journey the following morning, but that night it rained heavily again, and the difficult roads soothed the most urgent worries of most. The rainy season had started early and winter was now upon us. Surely no angry Chaldean army would pursue until winter had passed and the rains had eased?

No, there was no hurry: food was plentiful in Bethlehem and who would want to travel so far in such wintry weather?

Chapter 16

Another birthday

A day stretched into a week and one week into two, yet still we stayed in Bethlehem. The unseasonably heavy rain continued and the muddy roads were not inviting.

We saw no sign of the Chaldean army, and heard no worrying news either.

Winter settled in around us. Men and women relaxed and reflected on the momentous times that had overtaken them during the last year.

For me, it was a time of sombre thought as I reviewed the year that had closed so many chapters in my life. I was a priest, but now the temple in which I had worked was gone. I was a prophet, but the city and nation which had been the subjects of many of God's prophecies through me were gone. I had also been a prophet to many other nations, but my time for warning them had passed. Some had already felt the iron fist of Nebuchadnezzar, and the rest would do so soon. Ishmael's escape to the Ammonites would provide only a brief respite.

When leading us to Bethlehem, fear had prompted the field commanders to choose roads that did not take us near Jerusalem – just in case there were still some Chaldean soldiers left in the city. However, I wanted to see what remained of it, so two weeks later, I walked back to Jerusalem. The roads were deserted and significantly damaged by the heavy rain. I saw a surprising number of wild animals – it was as if all human inhabitants had been taken away and the country left to the animals.

Though I was familiar with the city from all angles, when at last it came in sight there was little to recognise. The once mighty walls were but scattered piles of rubble, and the gatehouses in which I had so often prophesied had been shattered and lay strewn across the roads they had guarded.

I made my way around the southern end of the city of David, through the Valley of Slaughter where the smell of decay still lingered. Across the Kidron I could see the remains of the Chaldean camps, with piles of debris strewn everywhere. Weeds and scrub were growing wild and free – already, in only two months, the hills looked different.

Centuries before, Abraham had obeyed God and come to Mount Moriah to make a sacrifice. On that occasion God, pleased with Abraham's faith, had provided the ram himself, but now the chosen mountain held only the fire-blackened ruins of God's house, a reminder of his rejection of the faithless worship of Abraham's descendants.

God had pleaded with Israel through hundreds of prophets over hundreds of years, yet his words had always fallen on deaf ears until there was no remedy.

The heavy rain had swollen the Kidron River, making crossing difficult. As I searched for a place to cross, I saw many cloth-covered corpses, and at times I nearly retched at the unbearable smell.

Eventually, I found a place where I could cross without getting too wet and climbed to the saddle by which I had so often approached the city from Anathoth. It was the view of Jerusalem with which I was most familiar, but now the difference was overwhelming.

Sitting down on a rock, I looked towards Jerusalem and I couldn't help it – I wept. After a while, I controlled my tears, but my emotions demanded some expression. When Josiah died, I had been driven to compose a lament that strove to express the unbearable loss the nation had suffered; now, the sight of Jerusalem as a silent ruin moved me even more powerfully. The words seemed to flow easily and it took little effort to arrange them as the start of an acrostic Hebrew poem:

> "How lonely sits the city
> that was full of people!
> How like a widow has she become,
> she who was great among the nations!
> She who was a princess among the provinces
> has become a slave.
> She weeps bitterly in the night,
> with tears on her cheeks;
> among all her lovers
> she has none to comfort her;
> all her friends have dealt treacherously with her;
> they have become her enemies.
> Judah has gone into exile because of affliction
> and hard servitude;
> she dwells now among the nations,
> but finds no resting place;
> her pursuers have all overtaken her
> in the midst of her distress."[90]

---

[90] Lamentations 1:1-3

Then I sat and thought and remembered. No-one came near me, and the only sounds were the birds flying purposefully south and the breezes that seemed to wander aimlessly around.

Forty years before, when I had approached Jerusalem for the first time as a prophet, I had seen a dilapidated temple, its buildings in urgent need of repair. This had been a true reflection of my people's attitude to God. They saw him as a God of the past, a God who had once been great but whose time was over.

Josiah had subsequently fought to overcome the idolatry and evil by directing the nation to the worship of God. He had made some progress during the rest of his reign, and an appearance of worship had spread through Judah. But the reformation had been shallow, and his attempts to effect genuine and permanent change had failed.

His sons had had none of the humble love of God that had lived in their father. During their reigns, all of Josiah's good work had been undone, whether by intent or by negligence.

And now Judah's false worship had led to destruction. For many years, the silence and peace of a true Sabbath rest would rule over the city in which God had once put his name.

As I pondered, I locked once more onto the questions that had so unsettled me in the time around the fall of Jerusalem. But now I had more evidence to consider, since the recent events in Mizpah.

Had Judah really deserved her punishment?

Had not death come cruelly and indiscriminately to young and old, rich and poor, male and female, slave and free? Was that fair?

Why had God brought such horrific judgement on his people? Punishment for the worship of idols and the utter disdain with which they had treated God's laws – that I could understand. But why had the punishment been so terrible? I had puzzled long over the question, worrying it like a dog gnawing at a bone, trying to understand.

Yet the disaster had *not* been completely indiscriminate: God had *not* killed everyone. Ebed-melech, a foreigner, had been promised his life, and he had survived. Baruch had been promised his life, and he too still lived. Zedekiah, the prisoner, was probably now in Babylon, but he had lived as God had said. I too had survived, despite my complaining and my nearness to some of the most horrific events.

There was too much evidence – far too much – that *God was in control* and would always fulfil his promises, but there was not enough information to allow me to understand his work. That was really my problem. How did God decide who should live and who should die; who should go into captivity and who should remain?

On a national level, the facts were easy to assemble.

God had assured us that he shows steadfast love to those who love him and keep his commandments.[91]

God had also assured us that he loved Israel because of the fathers.[92]

Obedience, he had promised, would earn rain and fertility. It had all been spelled out so simply:

"And if you will indeed obey my commandments
that I command you today, to love the Lord your God,
and to serve him with all your heart
and with all your soul,
he will give the rain for your land in its season,
the early rain and the later rain,
that you may gather in your grain

---

[91] Exodus 20:6; 34:6-7; Numbers 14:18-19; Deuteronomy 5:10; 7:9
[92] Deuteronomy 7:8; 10:15

and your wine and your oil.
And he will give grass in your fields for your livestock,
and you shall eat and be full.
Take care lest your heart be deceived, and you turn aside
and serve other gods and worship them;
then the anger of the Lord will be kindled against you,
and he will shut up the heavens,
so that there will be no rain,
and the land will yield no fruit,
and you will perish quickly off the good land
that the Lord is giving you."[93]

We had earned the promised punishments, yet God had not given us his judgement in full measure. Droughts had come, to be sure, but we had not perished as a nation. God had promised a returning remnant.

Habakkuk, another prophet of Yahweh, once complained about God's use of the Chaldeans to punish Judah, and God had responded by showing that in time the Chaldeans would also suffer for their behaviour.

The Chaldeans had attacked Judah with savage brutality – yet that brutality had been no different from the vicious attacks of my own nation against God's prophets and messengers throughout history. King Manasseh, the worst of the worst, had filled Jerusalem from one end to the other with the blood of the righteous, yet there had been no outcry from the people. Instead, they had joined in with relish. Now Ishmael had killed at least 120 men in Mizpah with savage brutality – how could I claim that the Chaldeans were any worse than my own people?

God balances national and personal rewards and punishments, and I had seen the evidence of that balance – in fact, I was part of it.

---

[93] Deuteronomy 11:13-17

Was I willing to accept that everything I had seen was justice? Could I acknowledge that this was God, in control, and showing love for thousands who would obey him?

This was probably my greatest test.

It was not that I thought mankind's ways were right: I had always felt there was far more evil than good in the ways of idolatrous mankind. I loved the righteousness that God demanded.

My problem was just that I wanted God to do things *my* way. My inconsistent, biased, illogical way.

I could acknowledge that God had been amazingly patient and gentle with my people – more than I wanted him to be in some cases. But I also knew that thousands had died in his judgement – and I had wanted him to be more gentle.

Yet it was not as if any of the death and suffering had come without warning. Had I not spent forty years warning people? Even near the very end, when the Chaldeans had been camped around the walls, God had given detailed warnings to King Zedekiah and set clearly before him the stark choice he faced. To the people also, he had given the open warning:

"Thus says the Lord:
'Behold, I set before you the way of life
and the way of death.
He who stays in this city shall die
by the sword, by famine, and by pestilence,
but he who goes out and surrenders
to the Chaldeans who are besieging you
shall live and shall have his life as a prize of war.' "[94]

So how could I complain? God had given people a choice and they had made their choice. Those who

---

[94] Jeremiah 21:8-9

trusted God had left the city and surrendered. The rest had chosen the way of death – and died for it. They did not trust God's promise, or believed that they knew better. And now those people could no longer sacrifice their children to Baal or Molech. They could no longer kill God's prophets, persecute the righteous and promote evil. No longer could they pursue a life of utter selfishness, oppressing widows, orphans and foreigners. Nor could they lead their surviving children, friends and neighbours into evil.

Maybe God knew what he was doing better than I did!

I did not know enough to judge, and I could not hope to do so. As a tiny and ignorant component in the vast scope of world events, all I could do was to accept that God knew what he was doing and that his way was best.

Winter deepened and the rain seemed to wash away the worries of the remnant – for the time being. Yet very few people seemed to consider the possibility of returning to Mizpah, and most of those who did were quickly talked out if it. The winter weather was their protection, but winter would not last.

Ebed-melech was an exception. Shortly after my visit to Jerusalem, he announced to me that he was going back to his farm. I was pleased and advised him not to wait any longer, but not to tell any of the leaders. The next morning, he came to say goodbye while I was out on the hills praying. He carried a small bundle of clothes and wore a big smile.

"Goodbye, Jeremiah, sir," he said. "I can't wait to get back to the new farm that God has given me. All of this rain will give wonderful crops in the spring and God has promised his care too – even if I'm not an Israelite."

"You'll be all by yourself on the farm and there will be very few people in the land," I replied, "but don't worry, God will still be with you."

"Before Ishmael did his worst, I was enjoying the freedom of life as a farmer and felt so thankful for Yahweh's care. It's a wonderful land he promised to Israel," he said, and shrugged his shoulders. "I can't understand why everyone wants to leave it."

He left, walking with a light step towards the road that would carry him north. I puzzled all over again as to why some people – in this case a foreigner – took God at his word and relaxed in his love, while most people could never give up control and trust God enough to fully obey him.

Winter began to recede as I finished a series of five laments over the destruction that had unfolded around me that year. They reflected on the events, but were not completely personal. Anyone who suffered through those times could name people who suffered the horrors I described, but the words will never have the same impact on others. I knew many of the priests who were killed in the temple, some of the young women who were raped in their homes, and many of the young men who were killed in the streets by Chaldean soldiers who played cat and mouse games with them. I could have put names in many of the stanzas, but instead I wrote in an ordered way, in the acrostic form used in many of our Psalms. For me, it kept the tears at bay and allowed me to write without being completely overcome.

As I wrote, I thought, and I still could never understand all of what had happened. Without God's knowledge and wisdom, I can never understand his actions.

Yet I was willing to accept that I had lived through a time that God had never wanted to have happen. God had always wanted Israel to walk with him as Abraham, Isaac and Jacob had done; to live in his love and the blessings he offered.

At least I did feel that I now understood more about God's plans and the purpose of the events in our lives. God is eternal and his plans for us can be also.

That thought led me back to thoughts about my family and others.

My father and Azariah my brother were both High Priests – a great responsibility. God would judge how each had done his job. Gemariah, my other brother, had suffered great sadness and responded with bitterness and anger. My mother alone had watched all of the events in our family and responded with faith and trust in God.

Josiah had shown great faith, but his end had been tragic. Ahikam had taught me many lessons, but had always kept God at arm's length, quarantining God's control over his life.

Miriam, Shobai and Maacah had lived among idolaters in Bethel, yet their happy and open faith had always encouraged me. God knew best, and he had never allowed Shobai and Maacah to grow old. I didn't know why, but I had learned that I didn't need to. When the branch, our Messiah, came, Abraham would inherit the land, and so would those who had a faith like his. I would see them again then.

Forty years as a prophet; forty years of delivering God's message when most would not listen; forty years of watching a tragedy slowly building, before rushing suddenly to its climax. Even God's patience had an end.

Finally, I asked myself the question: would I do it again? If I had known then what I know now and had to begin my forty years all over again, would I try to avoid it?

God thought it was worthwhile to send me even though he knew I would not succeed in changing the nations.

Nevertheless, those who would not listen had been warned again and again. God cared about that.

Those who had listened were like flames that sprang to life and burned fiercely with God's light in the darkness – and God welcomed them.

Yes. Since God had thought it necessary at the start, I would do it all over again.

CR

Winter drew to an end, and the question of what to do next became more pressing once again. With the end of the cold and rain, people began to think of spring and the new year. Everyone knew that armies would soon begin to move again – it was the time when kings went out to battle. Had the news of the massacre in Mizpah ever reached Chaldean ears? Whether it had or not, how soon might Chaldean soldiers arrive in the land?

Yet winter had brought reflection, and many had pondered the disaster that had befallen our nation and re-considered God's messages. Although in the aftermath of Gedaliah's assassination, everyone had fearfully agreed to run away to Egypt, a sizeable group were now pushing for the remnant of Judah to focus on Yahweh our God.

Since stopping at Chimham's Inn, the remnant had spread out through Bethlehem, filling all the empty houses. But the inn was still a gathering place, and I visited it often, trying to deliver God's latest messages and convince people that God's ways were the best ways. Baruch and I often discussed the words that God had spoken to me and tried to decide the best order for their compilation. God's extra words regarding the coming destruction of Babylon must also be fitted in and some more context added in places. One day, Baruch and I were sitting at our favourite table near the entrance, many scrolls spread out in front of us, when Johanan the son of Kareah came in. The day was cool but dry, and we could hear the sound of many voices outside as he opened the door, saw us and walked over.

"Jeremiah, you are a prophet of Yahweh and we need your help," he said. "Can you please come outside with me? We have a favour to ask you."

Baruch and I looked at each other and I think we were both somewhat concerned what this might mean. When you have been threatened and attacked several times, it leaves you a little cautious.

We both stood up and walked outside.

A large crowd was waiting for us, with Jezaniah and the other field commanders standing off to one side with their men.

I don't understand how people feel about prophets. I have been treated with great respect at times and utter contempt at others. Apparently this was a time for respect.

Jezaniah the son of Hoshaiah was the spokesman, and he promptly stepped forward and said to me, very politely, "Let our plea for mercy come before you, and pray to the Lord your God for us, for all this remnant – because we are left with but a few, as your eyes see us – that Yahweh your God may show us the way we should go, and the thing that we should do."

I am still an optimist, despite everything, so this request filled me with joy. The people wanted to know God's will so that they could obey it!

"I have heard you," I replied formally, but happily. "Behold, I will pray to Yahweh *your* God according to your request, and whatever the Lord answers you I will tell you. I will keep nothing back from you."

"May the Lord be a true and faithful witness against us if we do not act according to all the word with which the Lord your God sends you to us," replied Jezaniah. "Whether it is good or bad, we will obey the voice of the Lord our God to whom we are sending you, that it may be well with us when we obey the voice of the Lord our God."

The words were right, but my heart sank as I heard them. History shows that when people announce that they will follow God's word before they know what it is, they normally refuse to do so as soon as they find out. Still, I hoped that they had all learned the lesson and would keep their word this time. As I looked around at the crowd, there were many nodding heads and several shouts of "Amen."

Back in the inn, Baruch and I packed up our scrolls and I went immediately to pray, presenting my people's plea for mercy to God.

There was no immediate answer from God, but this was not unusual. At times God has answered my questions immediately, but much more often there has been a delay.

The days passed, and every day I was asked if the answer had been given. And with each passing day, it was easy to see that fear of the Chaldeans was growing, and probably doubt too.

It seemed that as soon as the question had been put to God, many of the people suddenly realised that they knew the answer they wanted. They also remembered the doubt with which they had heard my words before, and I suspect that they were wondering whether they should have asked at all.

I don't know if these facts are the reasons why God waited, but the delay certainly gave sufficient time for people's doubts and questions to grow and for everyone to realise what they *really* wanted. Many of the people seemed to reach the stage where the answer was just a given. Nobody had any doubt that God would give his stamp of approval to the proposed escape to Egypt.

CR

Ten days later it was my birthday, and during the night Yahweh spoke to me again. As on the first occasion, on my seventeenth birthday, the word of God came like the slow start of a fire, with light and heat. Somehow, the light was shining *inside* me and I could feel it growing brighter. Then the familiar voice came: expansive, vast, uncontained, filling my being and threatening to burst me open. Yet there was also a calm certainty that made any doubt impossible. These were the words I was to say to the people:

> "Thus says the Lord, the God of Israel,
> to whom you sent me to present
> your plea for mercy before him:
> If you will remain in this land,
> then I will build you up and not pull you down;
> I will plant you, and not pluck you up;
> for I relent of the disaster that I did to you.
> Do not fear the king of Babylon,
> of whom you are afraid.
> Do not fear him, declares the Lord,
> for I am with you, to save you
> and to deliver you from his hand.
> I will grant you mercy,
> that he may have mercy on you
> and let you remain in your own land."[95]

As I had expected, it was a message that guaranteed us safety and God's protection – if we stayed in Judah. It did not stop there, either: the results of ignoring God's instructions followed, in simple and compelling words.

---

[95] Jeremiah 42:9-12

Then the light and the voice faded and I felt the familiar urge to do something about it. I tried to ignore it, since there was really nothing I could do at that time, but it would not let me sleep, so I got up and wrote out the words on a scroll.

After I had finished, I reread what I had written and noticed that the words of condemnation and punishment were about three times as long as the blessings, in much the same way as the curses God had pronounced in the wilderness were so much longer than the blessings. It was clear to me then that God's answer would be rejected and the curse would come into play.

By that time it was nearly dawn and I went out to pray on the hillside near the town. I knew that it would be another difficult work-day – bread and butter for a prophet. Another case where people would have to choose between life and death, and would choose death. Things never seemed to get any better! I was glad that Ebed-melech had returned to his farm and would not be dragged down into Egypt as I expected to be myself.

When I got back, I summoned Johanan the son of Kareah and the other field commanders, and all the people. I wanted to make sure that everyone was present. The decision must be made in front of everyone. As they stood before me, I made the most of the powerful voice God had given me and presented to them God's direction that they should stay in the land God had given us. I presented God's guarantee of safety as compellingly as possible, but before I had even finished, the shouts and abuse were flying back at me.

"We're not staying here!" shouted a man.

"No, we will go to Egypt!" called another.

"In Egypt we won't see war or hear the sound of the trumpet," shouted a third.

God's promised blessings were roundly rejected. The

very men who had suggested that we should re-evaluate our attitude to Yahweh had promptly re-evaluated their own attitude and now had nothing to offer. No voices were raised in support of staying in the promised land, so I moved reluctantly on to God's curses.

"Hear the word of the Lord, O remnant of Judah.
'Thus says the Lord of hosts, the God of Israel:
If you set your faces to enter Egypt and go to live there,
then the sword that you fear shall overtake you
there in the land of Egypt,
and the famine of which you are afraid
shall follow close after you to Egypt,
and there you shall die.' "[96]

I delivered the words firmly, grimly, hoping to convince them of the terrible and certain trouble that their choice would bring – but I couldn't help feeling that everything was happening just the same as it always did. There were no signs of concern or repentance, just the brazen indifference that I had grown used to. Nevertheless, I continued with God's words:

" 'All the men who set their faces
to go to Egypt to live there
shall die by the sword, by famine, and by pestilence.
They shall have no remnant or survivor
from the disaster that I will bring upon them.
For thus says the Lord of hosts, the God of Israel:
As my anger and my wrath were poured out
on the inhabitants of Jerusalem,
so my wrath will be poured out
on you when you go to Egypt.' "[97]

"God's angry with us anyway," called a man from the back of the crowd. "This won't be any different. He hasn't ever loved us."

---

[96] Jeremiah 42:15-16
[97] Jeremiah 42:17-18

"We've survived his judgements anyway," came another voice from the front.

"We're meant to be his chosen people, and look what that has brought us."

"It's nothing to do with Yahweh anyway."

It seemed that the people had many different reasons for rejecting God's words, but they all wanted to reject them. I held up my hand for silence, and eventually it came. I had to make one final plea, a final warning, and announce God's final judgement:

"Know for a certainty that I have warned you this day that you have gone astray *at the cost of your lives*. For you sent me to the Lord your God, saying, 'Pray for us to the Lord our God, and whatever the Lord our God says declare to us and we will do it.' And I have this day declared it to you, but you have not obeyed the voice of the Lord your God in anything that he sent me to tell you. Now therefore know for a certainty that you shall die by the sword, by famine, and by pestilence in the place where you desire to go to live."[98]

They listened in silence until I finished, but the moment I did, there was a throng of people wanting to shout me down.

"You're telling a lie," said Azariah, the son of Hoshaiah.

"Yahweh our God did not send you to say, 'Do not go to Egypt to live there,' but Baruch the son of Neriah has set you against us," added Jezaniah his brother.

"Baruch wants to deliver us into the hand of the Chaldeans, so that they can kill us or take us into exile in Babylon," shouted Azariah.

---

[98] Jeremiah 42:19-22

Many others shouted abuse too, and the dismissive attitude of the crowd was summed up in a single sentence from Johanan as he came and stood in front of me with his hands on his hips.

"The Lord did not send you at all!" he said, pointing his finger at me accusingly.

With that, he turned away, and from then on I was excluded from the decision-making process. The field commanders and the other arrogant men led the discussion, and very soon it was agreed that we would all be going to Egypt: all of the remnant of Judah who had returned to live in the land of Judah from all the nations to which they had been driven, and all the men, women and children whom Nebuzaradan the captain of the guard had left with Gedaliah the son of Ahikam.

For some reason, they seemed to be sure that Baruch and I would cause trouble if we were left here, so we were both to be dragged along whether we liked it or not.

I was glad that Ebed-melech would not be forced to come and would be left to enjoy his reward from Yahweh for his faithfulness and courage.

That night, I began to write this diary, trying to set down in order the main events of the forty years I have spent as a prophet to the nations.

It turned out to be a massive job, though: much larger than I had ever imagined and taking much longer to write. It has shown some of my joys – there have been precious few of those – and some of my difficulties. Events have made life hard at times, but my main troubles have come from within. Personal emotions, and my questioning, first the patience, and then the judgements of God, have made my work much harder than it would have been if I had always maintained my confidence that God knows best.

The next morning, we left for Egypt.

Review

Have I failed as a prophet?

Most of those I spoke to did not take warning – was this failure?   Did not God warn Isaiah that he must prophesy

" 'Until cities lie waste
without inhabitant,
and houses without people,
and the land is a desolate waste,
and the Lord removes people far away,
and the forsaken places are many
in the midst of the land.
And though a tenth remain in it,
it will be burned again,
like a terebinth or an oak,
whose stump remains
when it is felled.'
The holy seed is its stump."[99]

Isaiah was just one of a line of prophets, and I have been the last in that line. I am the one who has seen the cities laid waste and the land made into a desolate waste. I have seen the burning again of the remnant as Ishmael killed so many of the few who had remained. Yet still I know that the holy seed will come – the branch from David, the king who will rule.

---

[99] Isaiah 6:11-13

But now I know with certainty that I will not see it until God's promise of resurrection is fulfilled.

In the meantime, I am not to be the last prophet. Away in Babylon, I know that Daniel and others are reporting the words of Yahweh to Jews and Chaldeans alike. Not only so, but sometime the great prophet like Moses must come. God's people and God's kingdom are not finished. Rather, one chapter has finished and a new chapter will begin when the seventy years of captivity ends.

I have watched so many people abandon God's way, and have come perilously close to doing so myself, yet God has never let me go. He never lets anybody go without a struggle, but he never forces anyone either. I have known so many who have heard God's word; considered it; even toyed with the idea of following it – but then turned away. It was as if they were about to go through a doorway into a better place when suddenly they heard a cry from behind offering them something they could not resist, or they realised that there were things they could not carry with them through the gate. So they turned aside and never entered.

Others – and what a frighteningly small number there have been – saw the doorway and rushed through it with a smile on their face, never looking back. They threw away their baggage outside the door and hurried on through, happy to go on without it.

But now my work in Judah is over. The nation is gone. Death has taken many and many have gone into captivity. The captives will return after seventy years, as God promised.

Through God's grace, a small remnant remained in the land, but now that remnant has rejected God's command and left. They – *we* – will never return.

About the author

Mark Morgan was born in Australia during 1963; the youngest son of Peter and Meryl Morgan. Deeply involved in religion all of his life, he has worked as a lay preacher, Sunday School teacher and missionary – trying to balance the many demands of spiritual life with those of family and paid employment.

After graduating, he worked in engineering for several years before concentrating on software development. Happily married and blessed with eight children, he has spent many years reading the Bible and learning to teach its lessons.

Writing Bible-based novels now fills much of his time.

Free Download

Paul in Snippets

A 109-page PDF novelette by Mark Morgan.

The life of Paul painted from the Acts of the Apostles.

Get your free copy of *Paul in Snippets* when you sign up for the Bible Tales mailing list. As well as the eBook, you will receive a weekly email newsletter with micro tales, informative articles and special offers.

Visit **https://www.BibleTales.online/free-pins**

www.BibleTales.online

Bible Tales Online

Other books by Mark Morgan are available from Bible Tales Online.

Terror on Every Side!

THE LIFE OF JEREMIAH

From a family of priests in the peaceful reign of good King Josiah, came a young man Jeremiah, bringing words from God to his people. It was no message for the fainthearted, either. It was a message of *Terror on Every Side!*

Volume 1 – Early Days
Volume 2 – As Good As It Gets
Volume 3 – Darkness Falling
Volume 4 – The Darkness Deepens
Volume 5 – No Remedy

Hard-cover, paperback, eBook and audiobook.

Micro-tales

Collections of short stories about Bible characters or events, available in paperback, eBook and audiobook.

Fiction Favours the Facts
Fiction Favours the Facts – Book 2

Other novels

Joseph, Rachel's son

Bible Tales Online continues to publish books.
To find the list of currently available books, visit

https://www.BibleTales.online/books

www.BibleTales.online